AMBUSH IN LIMBO

A chilling yell arose from the darkness. And forty-five wild-looking youths poured into the courtyard at a run.

They looked like demons. The dim glow of a distant streetlight illuminated their spiky white hair, their scarlet faces, and the razor edges of the handaxes that they brandished.

Cord saw, to his horror, that Samella had disappeared, lost somewhere in the shadows. But he could not search for her—because two Hatchetmen were bearing down on him, evil grins on their demonic faces. . . .

Bantam Books by Douglas Hill

Exiles of ColSec
The Caves of Klydor
ColSec Rebellion

For Polly
affectionately

Contents

1. The Inspectors   1
2. Leavetaking   10
3. Exiles   18
4. Itharac   27
5. Homecoming   34
6. The Metropolis   43
7. First Ambush   51
8. Stele   59
9. Second Ambush   68
10. Prisoners of Limbo   78
11. Flight to Disaster   87
12. Prisoners of ColSec   96
13. Death on the Streets   106
14. Escape from Earth   119
15. War on the Asteroid   129
16. Ultimatum   137
17. Pathfinders   149

1

The Inspectors

The broad, triangular shape of the spaceship floated through the upper atmosphere, above the planet Klydor. The orange sun reflected from its gleaming metal surface, brightly enough to be painful to the eye, had any eyes been watching. And upon that brightness were patches of coloured metal, letters that spelled a strange name: ColSec.

The spacious interior of the ship contained five people. Two of them sat together at one side of the control panel, studying images of the planet's surface that appeared on the screens of the ship's scanners. One of the two was a stringy, balding man with small spectacles, whose mouth was pinched in what looked like a permanent expression of disapproval. His companion was a middle-aged woman, taller and much broader, whose firm jaw suggested that she was used to giving orders and having them obeyed.

Both of them wore short, voluminous robes, colourful and luxurious. The others in the control room, three heavy-set men, wore uniforms of metallic blue cloth and dark leather, with guns holstered at their belts. One of the three, the pilot, sat hunched over the instruments of the panel. The other two, their helmets laid aside, lounged idly in reclining couch-seats, faces blank with boredom.

As the ship continued on its drifting way above the planet, the stringy man waved a hand at the screens.

"I see no reason to descend further," he said. "The scanners show no signs of human life. It is not likely that any of them survived."

The woman next to him went on studying the screens in silence. The images showed an expanse of forest—shadowy and alien. The trees had smooth trunks, crowned by upward-thrusting silvery leaves. Among the leaves, at the top of each trunk, was a strange bulge, like a large whitish fungus. In the dimness on the ground, under the trees, there seemed to be little undergrowth and no sign of movement.

But the part of the forest directly below the ship revealed a long, narrow clearing, where the grey-green turf was entirely bare of trees, save for broken stumps. It looked as if a gigantic scythe had swept down, slicing away the trees like stalks of grain. The clearing must have been formed some months earlier, for saplings had begun to sprout at the clearing's edge. But the observers in the spaceship had no concern with trees, young or old.

Their attention was fixed on the object at one end of the clearing—the object that had surely created that open area. It was a cylindrical metal shape that had once been a ColSec space shuttle, but was now a wreck.

The front section was crumpled and shattered, torn metal splaying out in all directions. Clearly the shuttle had crash-landed, hitting the forest at a flat, skimming angle, ploughing through the trees until it came to a halt. The shuttle's airlock was firmly closed, and as in the rest of the forest there was no sign of life around it.

The stringy man smirked over his glasses at the blue-uniformed pilot. "No need for Civil Defenders on this voyage," he said. "We seem to have come to inspect only corpses."

The pilot shrugged, not taking his eyes from his instruments. "Wouldn't be the first time," he muttered. "Sir."

The last word was added almost insolently, and the thin man's mouth pinched even tighter. But before he could speak, the woman nodded decisively.

"Certainly there are no survivors here, Muril," she said. "But let us not jump to conclusions. Remember the other object that the scanners showed."

"Of course, Reema," Muril replied. He waved a skinny hand grandly. "Pilot!"

Silently glowering, the pilot touched the controls. Smoothly, the great ship curved away. In seconds the forest, and the crumpled shuttle, were left behind. The ship soared above a broad valley, bisected by a winding river, and then—many kilometres further on—swept across a forbidding area of rocky hills scarred with steep ravines.

Beyond that area, the terrain changed again. It rose towards rolling uplands, where the thick grey-green turf reappeared, with plentiful thickets of brush and clusters of trees. But these were not the blade-leaved trees of the distant forest. Some were slender and gracefully bushy, others were tall and stately with enormous flat leaves.

Again the spaceship slowed into a drifting circle, then began a steeply angled descent, retro-jets flaring. It settled heavily to the ground about two hundred metres away from where a small rivulet gurgled down into a glade to form a clear pool, with feathery bushes growing abundantly on the banks.

The ship's airlock slid open and the three Civil Defenders stepped out warily—wearing their heavy helmets now, guns in their hands. Even more warily, Muril and Reema followed.

All five of them seemed indifferent to the beauty of the place—the warmth of the sunlit air, the music of the rivulet, the delicacy of the feathery brush. For a second they were startled, and their guns came up sharply, when a fluting chirrup sounded among the treetops. Then a host of small flying things, bright yellow, with wings as delicate as the brush, fluttered out of a tree—their chirruping calls continuing as they swirled in the air like falling petals from some enormous golden flower.

Ignoring them, the five humans moved forward. And now all their attention was fixed on the one object, within all that alien beauty, that was entirely out of place.

Near the pool, at the edge of the glade, stood a machine. It was more or less cylindrical, about half as tall again as a man, standing upright on angled metal legs.

Reema regarded the machine as she had regarded the landscape, with distaste. "Pilot," she snapped, "take your men and investigate. *Carefully.* Try not to disturb anything. Inspector Muril and I will wait here until you have examined the interior."

The three Civil Defenders looked at each other, grimaced, then strode swiftly towards the machine.

"It is of course a standard escape module from a ColSec ship," Reema said briskly, as if offering instruction. "No doubt one of our pilots has been stranded here. Perhaps he is still alive."

As she spoke, the Civil Defenders had reached the machine. One of them cautiously opened the module, then stepped inside, vanishing from view. The other two appeared to relax, lowering their guns.

Reema nodded with satisfaction. "It seems to be secure. Come, Muril."

They began to move away, passing between a dense thicket of brush and a clump of the tall, stately trees. But then they paused. From the huge leaves of one tree, above them, they heard a sudden low sound, like a choking growl.

As they jerked their heads up, Muril turned white, his scrawny throat working as panic stifled the scream rising within him. Reema, just as pale, could only give a strangled bleat of terror. They stood rooted, staring at the grotesque mass of alien horror slithering down the tree towards them.

There were four creatures, looking like a combination of oversized porcupines and giant slugs. Each massive, humped body was nearly two metres across, covered with stubby spines. Small claws glittered around the flattened edge of each body, which curved inwards to cling to the tree. And as they reached the ground, their broad heads were thrust forward, mouths half-open to reveal rows of evilly stained fangs.

Two hundred metres away, the Civil Defenders stood with their backs turned, unaware of the monsters. They did not hear Muril's whimper, or Reema's muffled gurgle of terror. Nor did they hear the new chorus of soft growls, as the four horrors slithered jerkily towards the humans, claws gouging the turf.

But in that moment the air was split by a searing hiss. A pencil-line of fiery light lanced out of the thicket next to Muril and Reema. It stabbed into the ground in front of the monsters. And the creatures wheeled and fled, in a frantic slithering scuttle, as flame erupted from the turf.

Muril sank to his knees, as if his legs had given way. But Reema, trembling, turned—to see a man step out of the thicket, a laserifle cradled casually in one arm.

The man seemed to be in his early thirties, slim and wiry, wearing the remains of a silvery jumpsuit that was ragged and oddly stained. He had fair hair and piercing blue eyes, which held a glint that might have been mockery, or dislike, or both.

"Why didn't you shoot to kill?" Reema demanded, when she finally found her voice.

"No need," the man said easily. "They're vegetarians, leaf-eaters. Harmless, unless they feel threatened."

By then Muril had also regained the power of speech. "You were in those bushes all along!" he said accusingly, as he scrambled to his feet.

The man with the rifle nodded. "Seemed safer." He gestured towards the three Civil Defenders, who had become aware of the commotion and were running towards them. "Your men looked like they might shoot first and ask for ID after."

Reema snorted. "Certainly not—unless they were told to do so." Her eyes narrowed. "Presumably you are the pilot who landed here in the escape module?"

The man nodded, but before he could speak again Muril had stepped closer, peering at him. "I know you!" he announced. "You're Bren Lathan, one of ColSec's best space explorers!"

"I'm Lathan," the man agreed coldly.

"There was quite an outcry when you were reported to be lost in space," Muril went on. "ColSec will be pleased to know that you have survived."

"I'm sure," Lathan said dryly. "And I suppose you're the inspectors, come to check on the colony that should have been set up here on Klydor?"

As he spoke, he stepped casually away from the thicket, in the direction of the ship. The others turned to follow his movement—so that when Lathan paused again, the other five were standing with their backs to the thicket from which Lathan had appeared.

"We are indeed," Reema was saying. "I am Inspector Reema and this is Inspector Muril." She sniffed. "But our presence is clearly not required. We saw the wrecked shuttle before we landed here."

"Unfortunate," Muril put in. "It seems an excellent planet for a colony." He smirked. "But we can always find another shipload of those people to send here. There is no shortage of their kind on Earth."

"I don't suppose anyone survived the shuttle crash?" Reema asked indifferently.

"In fact some did," Lathan said. The glint of mockery had vanished from his eyes, leaving nothing but cold anger. "Five of the kids survived. And they're still very much alive, in spite of having spent months on this planet with almost no supplies or equipment."

"Really," Reema said, in the same tone of disinterest. "Where are they now?"

Lathan's grin was fierce and mirthless. "Why, they're right behind you, inspector," he said. "With a sun-gun."

2
Leavetaking

Expressions that mingled shock, disbelief and outrage appeared on the faces of the five ColSec people. They started to turn—but Bren Lathan's voice struck at them like a whip.

"Don't move!"

They froze—but it was not only Lathan's order that halted them. They had seen that other people were indeed emerging from the thicket where Lathan had hidden.

In the forefront was a broad-shouldered youth with a tangled thatch of red hair. He wore plain brown trousers and boots, with a bright sleeveless shirt that revealed the solidity of powerful muscle. His expression was grim and threatening—almost as threatening as the muzzle of the heavy weapon in his hands.

He strode across the turf to join Lathan, and with him came a slim girl with tawny blonde hair, who had a crude knife thrust into her belt. Behind her appeared three other young people, similarly dressed, in their late teens like the first two—but otherwise startlingly different.

One was a short, sturdy girl with wiry black hair bristling up from her scalp. Her face was oddly darkened with what looked like broad stripes of black paint, across her forehead and down her cheeks. With her were two boys, one tall and coffee-coloured, the other short with an ivory sheen to his skin. The heads of both were entirely hairless, bearing strange ridged scars that formed letters—R for the tall boy, J for the smaller one. And each of them had a small "s", made of silvery metal, embedded in the skin of his forehead.

These three teenagers carried spears, made from slim poles and shards of bright metal. And their expressions, too, were threatening—though there was a hint of mocking laughter in the eyes of the shorter boy.

The muscular redhead faced the ColSec group and levelled his heavy gun. "You CeeDees," he said sharply, "throw your weapons away from you."

The three Civil Defenders hesitated. Their faces twisted with brutal fury, as if they were on the verge of explosive action. But Lathan's laserifle swung up, to point at the face of Inspector Reema.

"That *is* a sun-gun," Lathan snapped, "and he knows how to use it. And I'm quite willing to take off the top of the inspector's head, if I have to."

"Do what they say!" Reema ordered, with more anger than fear in her voice.

Snarling, the CeeDees flung their weapons several paces away, on to the soft turf. The two hairless boys and the black-faced girl sprang to gather them up, dropping their spears.

"Nice," said the shorter boy, examining his weapon. "Electrical stunner, looks like."

"With a charge big enough to kill, at full power," his tall companion growled.

The smaller boy grinned at the ColSec group. "Don't tempt me."

The others laughed, except for the stocky redhead. He was still staring fixedly at the ColSec group, a look of almost hungry hatred in his eyes. His name was Cord MaKiy, and he had every right to hate any representative of ColSec—as had the other four teenagers, who had been exiled on Klydor ever since the crash-landing of their shuttle, months before.

Lathan gestured with his rifle at the CeeDees. "We'd better check them for other weapons."

"I'll do it," said the blonde girl, stepping forward calmly.

"Spread out around 'em," said the taller of the hairless boys. "Keep 'em covered, so they don't try to grab Samella."

They shifted positions, and the blonde girl, Samella, coolly conducted the search. She found some ugly little truncheons and some equally ugly wrist restrainers, in the belts of the CeeDees. She totally ignored the even uglier muttering and glares from the three men.

Reema was glaring even more furiously. "I don't know what you people are planning," she snarled, "but you cannot believe you will get away with it. The penalty for what you have done is death."

"What penalty isn't," Cord said fiercely, "where you come from?"

"We'll even make it easy for you," Samella said, "by introducing ourselves. I'm Samella Connel, from the north-west of the American Segment, and that's Cord MaKiy, a Highlander from northern Britain."

"Heleth," growled the black-faced girl, "from the Vampires troop of the Bunkers, under Old London."

"An' I'm Rontal," said the taller of the hairless boys, "an' he's Jeko. Free Streeters, from a place called Limbo. I reckon you know where Limbo is."

"So here we are, inspectors," Jeko said, with a wicked grin. "We been waitin' for you—'cause we knew that ColSec always checks on the kids they throw away into space. Sorry we got no colony goin' here on Klydor, with lotsa goodies to make ColSec even richer. But we had some problems here since we crashed."

"Only now," Heleth said menacingly, "it's you that's got the problems."

"They're going to kill us, Reema!" Muril quavered. "They're going to shoot us down!"

"Get hold of yourself, you idiot!" Reema raged.

"We're not going to kill you," Cord said. He spoke quietly, but there was a flintiness in his voice that silenced even Reema. "It would be simpler if we did, and maybe smarter. But that's what people like *you* would do. Not us. No, we're going to put you someplace where ColSec won't find you, and where you won't want to be—on your own, with no hope of escape or rescue. Just like ColSec did with us, and with all the other kids you've shipped out into space to make your colonies."

"You're going to... maroon us?" Muril said, trembling. "We'll die!"

"We'll leave you some basic supplies," Lathan told him. "It'll be up to you if you survive or not. Just like it was up to these young people, here on Klydor. And we'll worry about you just as much as ColSec worried about them." He gestured with the laserifle. "Now let's get to the ship."

Soon the spaceship was being prepared for departure. The ColSec people had been placed in body restrainers, which clamped their arms to their bodies, and were tucked away on couch-seats in the large passenger area of the ship. Lathan was at the controls, and the five teenagers were gathered at the airlock, gazing quietly out.

Cord was only then realizing fully what a wrench it would be to leave Klydor. From the very beginning, when they had survived the crash-landing, Cord had been determined to make the alien planet into *home*. He and his friends had, after all, wanted to create a colony—not for ColSec but for themselves. Now, he knew, though they had been on Klydor for only a few months, they had succeeded, even beyond their dreams.

Klydor *was* home, despite all the dangers and terrors that they had met. For Cord, it had become as much of a home as the mountains and glens of the Highlands, where he had spent all his life until being exiled by ColSec. And even though he knew that he might—with luck—soon be seeing the Highlands again, he felt a deep sense of loss at leaving Klydor.

But part of that feeling, he suspected, might come from the fact that a great many more dangers and terrors awaited them where they were going.

The others, staring silently out of the ship, seemed to be feeling the same way. And it was tall Rontal who put their thoughts into words.

"Seems funny," he said, "after all the times this place's tried to kill us—but I'm really sorry to be leavin'."

"Just our luck," Jeko said, for once without a grin. "We finally find a nice place to live on Klydor, and we gotta leave it."

Heleth poked him with a muscular finger. "Who's been moaning about being *bored*, ever since we found this place?"

Jeko looked at her innocently. "I never said I

was bored. I just said we should look around some more, find a little action."

As the others laughed mockingly, Jeko grinned. "Anyways," he went on, "ol' Heleth's prob'ly glad to be leavin'. She's not been happy since we made her come outa those caves."

"I don't think any of us is glad to be going," Samella interrupted, before Heleth's growl could become a reply. "And I think I'm going to miss GUIDE as much as anything."

GUIDE was a small navigational and data-storage computer that they had salvaged from the wreck of their shuttle. Over the months, it had come to seem like another member of the group. But there was no point in taking GUIDE where they were going, so they had placed the computer inside the now sealed escape module, safe from intruders.

"GUIDE will be here when we get back," Cord said, as if reassuring himself as much as the others. "The whole planet will be here when we get back."

"If," Jeko muttered.

But the others ignored the word. They had talked it all out, time and again. They knew what lay ahead of them, and how likely it was that they would not survive it. But for this moment they wanted to believe that it *was*, really, just a matter of time before they would be landing again amid the serene beauty of this part of Klydor.

Samella sighed. She had caught Lathan's eye, and the pilot had beckoned to them. The ship was ready—there was no more time to linger.

"Time to go," she told the others. They stepped back from the airlock, which hissed softly as it closed.

Moments later, the engines blazed out their fiery power. Gracefully, the ship rose, wheeling away into Klydor's orange sky—to begin the first stage of a voyage that would finally bring the exiles home.

3

Exiles

"There it is," Bren Lathan said.

Reluctantly Cord took his gaze away from the viewport—from the blazing, tumultuous kaleidoscope that had surrounded the ship for two days—and saw that the others were studying a large screen above the control panel.

Cord blinked at it. The shapes on the screen meant nothing to him. Samella was nodding, but then she was an expert in computers and advanced microtronics. Even the other teenagers knew enough about technology to make sense of what they were seeing. But to Cord, the wild Highlander, most technology was as strange as the alien life of Klydor.

Lathan saw Cord's difficulty. "That's a projection of this sector of space," he explained. "And there—" his finger touched a point of light on the screen—"is where we'll drop off our passengers, in an hour or so."

Cord shook his head wonderingly. His brain knew very well that their ultra-modern spaceship was moving so far beyond the speed of light that it was no longer affected by the laws of nature that governed the ordinary universe. It was the departure from "real" space that created the swirling storm of colour around the ship. But all of Cord's instincts and senses stubbornly told him that the ship seemed to be suspended, immobile, going nowhere at all.

He sighed as the others began talking about the re-entry into real space, orbital angles, and similar things. He let his gaze drift back to the riotous envelope of colour around them. And his mind drifted, too, back to thoughts of his first flight through space, many months before.

On that flight, a dozen teenagers including Cord had been despatched—by ColSec—to the wild planet Klydor. But something went wrong, and their ship crashed. Only six of the twelve survived the crash, and at once they met more threats to their survival. One of the six was killed, but Cord and his four friends fought their way through a host of dangers, until at last they could set out to explore Klydor.

And throughout all the terrors they had faced, they had not forgotten who their real enemies were— the arrogant, ruthless people who had flung them into exile on an alien world.

ColSec. Colonization Section. One of the most

powerful sections of the monstrous Organization that had ruled Earth since the devastations of the Virus Decades.

For most people on Earth, life under the Organization was near slavery, where any dissent was savagely punished. Yet, surprisingly, a few small groups did manage to find a freedom of sorts, in less desirable corners of the world—like the Highlands or the dustbowl of the northwest American plains where Samella's family had lived.

But others won some freedom in the very heartland of the Organization. These were the juvenile gangs, masters of the crumbling centres of once-great cities. Like Jeko's and Rontal's Streeters, in the wastelands at the heart of the Chicago-Detroit metropolis, in the American Segment. Or like the eerie, black-faced Vampires, Heleth's troop, who roamed the underground Bunkers beneath the streets of Old London.

Even the Civil Defenders, who enforced the Organization's cruel laws, could not wipe out the gangs. The young outlaws were too much at home in their tangled urban mazes. But the Cee Dees knew that the gangs were no threat to the Organization's rule. And in any case they were a useful source of manpower—for ColSec.

Any gang members caught by the Cee Dees were shipped off to faraway planets that could support human life. If they survived, ColSec had new colonies, new sources of wealth. If they did not survive, no one cared. There were always plenty more where they came from.

On Klydor, Cord and his friends vowed that they would make this new world their *own*, free from ColSec's control. They sought ways to protect it when, as they knew would happen, the ColSec inspectors came to claim the new colony. But, first, Bren Lathan landed on Klydor in an escape module from his wrecked ship. And behind him, in hot pursuit, came a team from a special CeeDee force known as the Crushers.

Crushers were highly trained killers whose job it was to erase, murderously, any stirrings of opposition to the Organization. Yet the five teenagers and Lathan fought them—and finally defeated them. Then Lathan revealed why the Crushers had been pursuing him.

He was a leader of a rebellion against ColSec, being organized among all the colonies on alien worlds. And he calmly told the five friends that they could have a crucial role to play in that rebellion.

At first it had seemed impossible, to Cord and the others. But during the time of waiting for the ColSec inspectors to visit Klydor, Lathan had outlined the rebels' plan, with a confidence that made it seem less and less like a foolish dream.

"We're not trying to free Earth," Lathan had told them. "We just want to free the colonies. And we have a lot of leverage. ColSec *needs* the colonies and the wealth that pours out of them."

"Right," Cord had said. "So it'll fight to keep them."

Lathan had shrugged. "We're going to give ColSec an ultimatum. Give us our freedom, our right to run our own lives—or we'll destroy everything that we've built on the colony worlds." He had smiled dryly. "ColSec will know exactly how much it would cost to rebuild the colonies from nothing."

"An' you'll have ColSec spaceships comin' at you 'fore you can turn round," Rontal had growled.

"They can't get to the planets that fast," Lathan had replied. "Remember, the colonies are widely scattered. And we have something that ColSec doesn't know about—some of their spaceships, which they believe were 'lost' in space."

"Like the inspectors' ship is gonna get lost," Jeko had said with a grin.

"Exactly," Lathan had said. "So we won't just wait around to be picked off by a ColSec fleet, one planet at a time. We'll *abandon* the colonies, and join together on a different planet to make a stand— if we have to."

"You'll have to," Heleth had said. "Wherever you go, ColSec'll come after you."

"Maybe," Lathan had said calmly. "But first a ColSec fleet would run into our ships—not many of them, but well-armed. Then they'd have to fight us on our home ground—a planet that we'll know a lot better than they do. It'll mean a long, drawn-out fight—and the supply lines for the ColSec fleet will be millions of light-years long. When ColSec realizes

all that, they should also see that such a space war
would cost as much as the loss of the colonies. It
could bankrupt them."

"And you want the rebels to make their stand
on *Klydor* . . ." Cord had said.

"They hadn't found a planet to be their base,
before," Lathan had said. "I know they'll agree that
Klydor is just right. A wild planet, with lots of rough
country where the defenders can live off the land—as
you five have."

But Samella had been frowning. "The *timing* is
wrong. As soon as ColSec gets your ultimatum—and
rejects it, as it surely will—it'll send out its spacefleet.
So when the rebels set off for Klydor, after destroying
the colonies, they'll be wide open to attack before
they can set up any defences here!"

Lathan had merely smiled. "Defences will already have been set up," he had said. "Secretly,
before our ultimatum goes out."

The rebels, he went on, planned to recruit a
small but special *army*, to be placed on Klydor in
advance—so they could get things ready to defend
the planet if ColSec attacked.

And, Lathan had announced, the rebels intended to recruit that army from a ready-made supply of
skilled guerrilla warriors—the teenage gangs of Earth.

"The rebels were having problems deciding who
to send to Earth," Lathan had said. "But you five
will be the solution. You're the ideal recruiters."

For Cord, that part of the plan had been the
most startling. It was shock enough to think that he

might see Earth again. But the idea that he and his friends would return to Earth secretly, trying to remain undetected while recruiting a rebel army under the noses of the Organization...

"It's the only way," Lathan had said. "There aren't enough people on the colonies to provide that army. But there are, in the gangs on Earth. I'm sure they'll join us, if you can get to them. And I think if anyone can, you can. You're tough and smart and lucky—and you're *survivors*." He had paused sombrely. "You'll need to be, back on Earth."

The five had been stunned—but they had agreed at once. They had no illusions about the dangers they would face, the fearsome odds against success. But no risk would be too great, they felt, if they had a chance to strike a blow against ColSec.

And now, Cord thought, as their ship streaked through the flowering streams of colour beyond "real" space—now, it has begun.

"There it is," Lathan said, as he had before.

The ship had emerged from the flaming brilliance, to re-enter real space, surrounded by the icy gleams of countless stars. Around the nearest of those stars revolved the planet that was their goal.

"What's this world called?" Heleth asked.

Lathan glanced at the prisoners, huddled on their couch-seats, and grinned as if at a private joke. "Tell you later," he said mysteriously.

"Hope it's a *bad* place," Jeko said eagerly. "Lotsa monsters and stuff."

"I don't know about monsters," Lathan said. "But our friends won't find it cosy."

"Good," Heleth said vindictively. Then they all fell silent, as the ship swung towards the bright sphere of the planet.

Soon the ship was settling, in a cloud of gritty dust, on to the most unappealing plain that Cord had ever seen. A biting wind swept the dust along in powdery drifts, piling it against the only things that interrupted the flat bleakness—heaps of stark boulders and patches of gnarled brush with black, thorn-edged leaves.

"Cold and nasty and ugly," Jeko said with relish. "These folks oughta be right at home."

Quickly they unloaded a few supplies, including food, clothing and a medi-kit—what every group of young exiles received from ColSec, to start life on a wild alien world. Lathan was also leaving the laserifle—Jeko and Heleth had objected, but were out-voted—but it would be taken apart, needing to be reassembled before being used. Finally the prisoners were herded out of the ship, upper bodies still held by the restrainers.

Muril and Reema stared at the landscape with horror, and even the stolid CeeDees looked stricken. "You *can't* leave us here!" Muril shrilled.

"You can survive," Lathan said coldly. "If you're tough enough."

"Build yourself a nice colony," Jeko said brightly. "Make ColSec proud of you."

As Muril subsided, moaning, Lathan moved to

unfasten his restrainer, so that Muril could free the others after the ship had taken off. And then Reema, shaking with fear and fury, found her voice.

"You won't get away!" she raged. "Wherever you're going, you can't escape! You fools—outer space *belongs* to ColSec! We are the *masters* of space! There is nowhere you can hide that ColSec cannot find you! And when we do, you will all wish that you *had* died on Klydor!"

4

Itharac

Reema's voice was rising into a scream, still hurling threats and dire promises as Lathan and the teenagers returned to the ship.

Jeko snickered. "Masters of space, she says. ColSec's got a lotta surprises comin'."

"They just had one, though they don't know it," Heleth said with satisfaction.

"They'd better not find out for a while yet," Lathan said firmly. "The Organization already has a vague idea that something is stirring in the colonies— that's why the Crushers came, looking for ringleaders, and ended up chasing me. But no one on Earth knows the extent of the stirring." His blue eyes surveyed them. "*Everything* hinges on that fact—that ColSec doesn't know there's a real, organized rebellion. Right now, secrecy is our best weapon, keeping the Organization unsuspicious while you're on Earth. One slip, one bit of bad luck..."

"And we're finished," Samella concluded.

Cord and the others nodded gravely, but Jeko was twitching. "Let's not sit here talkin' about bein' finished," he said. "Let's go get started!"

Lathan smiled and reached for the controls. "Right," he said. "We'll visit a colony."

"How far is it?" Cord asked.

"A few minutes away—on this planet," Lathan replied, grinning as they gaped at him. "The inspectors think they're on a wild planet—and so it is, over most of its surface. But its name is Itharac, and it's the first planet ColSec ever colonized. The colony is in a nicer area, halfway around the planet from here."

"Smart," Rontal said as the others burst out laughing. "Who'd look for lost inspectors on a colony world?"

Moments later, the ship was flashing through the upper atmosphere, towards the colony. And when they landed, the colonists greeted Lathan with joyful astonishment—for all the rebels believed that he had been captured or killed by the Crushers. The five young people were also warmly welcomed, and they were all whisked away for some intense talking. The rebels had feared that their intentions might have been discovered, if Lathan had been captured—and so everything had come to a standstill. But now, with secrecy intact, the rebel plans could go ahead.

So Cord and his friends saw little of the colony—

just a general impression of neat though primitive buildings in the midst of rolling fields of vivid yellow plants. The plants provided a valuable anti-biotic, for which ColSec paid the colony a cruelly low price—just as it exploited all the colony worlds and their resources.

A day of hectic discussions later, the plans were complete, and it was time for Lathan and the teenagers to leave again—in the ship they had taken from the inspectors. And two other ships—from the small fleet that the rebels had secretly acquired from ColSec, in the same way—would go with them.

The rebels intended to set up a temporary, hidden base somewhere in the solar system near Earth. The first groups of recruits for the army of Klydor would be ferried to that base by Lathan, one group at a time. The other two rebel ships would then carry them, all together, over the far longer distance to Klydor.

But Lathan himself would bring the last group of recruits from Earth. Those were to be from the Streeters, Jeko's and Rontal's troop. Lathan would take them, along with Cord and his friends, direct from Earth to Klydor.

Providing nothing went wrong . . .

It had been decided to set up the temporary base in the Asteroid Belt, beyond Mars, where ColSec mining operations had hollowed out the interiors of many asteroids. The rebels knew, from Lathan and other space explorers, that the asteroids were mostly automated, with robot workers and only a few human overseers. So there would be life-support within their interiors, but no serious resistance when the rebels took one asteroid over. And ColSec would not be alerted, since it rarely made direct contact with the asteroids, as long as the robots kept producing the ore.

Lathan was also sure that no one would be alerted or made suspicious by the various landings he would make on Earth, to drop off the five teenagers and then later to pick up the recruits. He would be in a ColSec ship, landing mostly at night in deserted places. Even if the ship was seen, no one would suspect that it was not on official ColSec business.

"That's one of our weapons, too, aside from secrecy," Lathan had said. "The fact that the Organization thinks it is *invulnerable*. They'd never dream that anyone would try what we're trying."

The five teenagers were not overly reassured to know that they could rely only on secrecy, the speed of their operation and, in part, on the Organization's smug belief that there could be no real threat to its power. But their doubts did not lessen their determination—to go to Earth to complete their mission.

Shortly, they were saying goodbye to the Itharac colonists and entering the spaceship. The teenagers were dressed as before, and Cord and Samella were also unarmed, hoping to survive by stealth rather than combat. But the other three had strapped knives to their forearms, claiming that among their own kind on Earth they would be undressed without weapons.

The great ship leaped into the sky, and moments later was surrounded by the bursting blooms of colour that signalled the entry into faster-than-light travel. For the next two days, again, Cord remained mostly near a viewport, gazing raptly out—except when he was gulping dull meals of food concentrate, or snatching a few hours of restless sleep. And most of that time, with the others, he was absorbed in nerve-grinding thoughts of what lay ahead, when they set out on their danger-filled journeys, on Earth.

Cord would be seeking recruits in the Highlands, and Samella would go with him—since she knew there was no hope of finding warriors among the poor dirt farmers of her homeland. At the same time, Heleth would be in the Bunkers, and Rontal and Jeko wanted to go with her, out of curiosity. Finally, all five would try to make their way together to Limbo, the home of the Streeters.

The Streeters were the largest gang of the American Segment, perhaps of all Earth, numbering over three hundred. If a large number joined the guerrilla army on Klydor, that force would be assured of being a suitable size. But to reach Limbo the five teenagers would have to cross the largest metropolis in the Segment, where droves of CeeDees patrolled the streets, where every step they took could plunge them into disaster.

And when the ship returned to "real" space, hurtling towards the dot of light that was Earth's sun, Cord knew that nothing he had ever experienced—

not even the worst moments on Klydor—had made him feel as coldly frightened as he felt just then.

The ship swept on, arrowing past the sun towards the luminous sphere that was Earth. All too soon, Lathan had manoeuvred it into orbit, then was sending it screaming down in a steep descent towards the planet's night-side. The first landing was to be in a sparsely inhabited, forest area near the outskirts of Old London, where some of the Bunkers' longest tunnels stretched out into the countryside.

Soon the ship was thunderously lowering itself to the ground, amid darkness and a slight drizzle from heavy clouds. It settled on to the wet grass and the airlock slid open. For a moment the five Klydoreans looked at each other, unable to find anything suitable to say.

"Remember," Lathan broke in quietly, "I'll be back two nights from now. But I won't land unless the scanners show you're here." He paused briefly. "Try to make it."

"We'll be all right," Heleth said. She scowled at Cord. "It's you I worry about. You sure your Highlanders can keep a secret?"

Cord glowered. "They don't like the Organization any more than the Vampires do. They won't betray us."

Heleth nodded, then grinned as the two Streeters raised their hands in a half-salute. "Right," she said. "See you."

They slipped out of the airlock, vanishing at once in the rainy night. Peering after them, Cord could see no sign that any living creatures existed in that darkness.

If any of them would make it, he thought to himself, it would be Heleth. The youths of the Bunkers, in their lightless tunnels, had developed the night vision and hearing of nocturnal animals. No one was better equipped than Heleth for furtive travelling by night. And she and the boys would be safe once they got into the Bunkers.

Then the airlock closed, and the ship rose again into the murky clouds—swinging northwards, to take Cord MaKiy home.

5

Homecoming

The village was no more than a handful of low stone cottages and a few rickety sheds, huddled in the lee of a heather-clad hill. A traveller might easily have passed it by without knowing it was there. But Cord knew it well, just as he knew all that area, and had gone straight to it after he and Samella had left the spaceship.

Even so, the journey—from the wilderness spot where Lathan had dropped them—took the rest of the night, so that they reached the village in the grey light of early morning. By then they were weary and hungry, drenched from walking through rain-sodden ferns and brush, shivering despite the insufoil space blankets clutched round their shoulders. Yet such feelings were as familiar to Cord as the terrain, where he had wandered many a time with the footloose uncle who had raised him.

Yet despite that heart-tugging sense of rightness that every traveller feels upon coming home, there was a strangeness, too, that saddened Cord. Until he was sixteen he had known only the storm-swept Highland landscapes, and had been content. But now, knowing other landscapes on an immeasurably distant world, he felt—with a sense of loss like a physical pain—that he no longer entirely belonged to these mountainous wilds.

Still, he had a job to do, and the village was where he would do it. He and his uncle had visited the village often, and he had many friends there—if they were still friendly.

As they moved closer to the cluster of cottages, Samella's teeth were chattering. "I'd think most of your people would be glad to join us," she muttered, "just to get out of this climate."

Cord grinned, thinking of the heavy wool plaids and furs that had kept him warm during his childhood. But before he could reply, they had entered the village and found a brawny youth wielding an axe on a heap of firewood.

The axe slipped from his hands as the youth stared. "Cord MaKiy!" he roared. "Where in fury did you spring from?"

Cord laughed at his pop-eyed amazement. "Donal," he said. "I'm glad to see you." He introduced Samella, laughing again as big Donal gazed at

her with open admiration that brought a tinge of
pink to her cheeks.

"We heard you had a fight in the city, Cord,
and were arrested," Donal said. "Was it not
true?"

"It was," Cord said. "And since then I've trav-
elled farther than you can imagine. But now I'm
back, with something to say to you and everyone.
And something to ask."

"You'll be welcome," Donal said, looking at him
curiously. "Come to the house."

Shortly, Cord and Samella had been abundantly
fed by Donal's smiling mother, and were dozing by a
cheery fire. But they were brought back to wakefulness
as the news of their arrival spread and other villagers
began to crowd into the cottage. Some came to bid
Cord welcome, others merely to stare at his strange
clothing and his "foreign" companion. And when
enough of them had gathered, Cord began to tell his
story.

A few of the older folk could barely conceive of
what he was talking about—alien planets, ColSec
colonies, rebellion in space. These were people who
knew little about the outside world on Earth, let
alone the galaxy. But, as patiently as he could, Cord
talked on—aided by Samella's fund of knowledge.
And he could see gleams of excited interest growing
in the eyes of some of his listeners, especially Donal
and the young people.

Among others his story stirred a different reaction. "It sound like a tale," one burly man finally

scoffed. "Like the tales of ghouls and goblins we tell the little ones."

Cord's patience gave way. He began to rise, bristling, ignoring Samella's attempts to restrain him. But Donal's grey-haired father raised an authoritative hand.

"It's no tale," he said. "I knew Cord and his uncle for many a year, and neither ever spoke a dishonest word." He glanced at Cord dourly. "But what I ask is—what has it to do with us? Why should Highlanders leave their homes to travel in space and fight a war against an enemy we know little of?"

Donal and the other teenagers might have replied, but it was Donal's mother who spoke first.

"Look at the young people for your answer, man," she said sharply. "And look at the past. They will go as their forefathers went. To find adventure, to seek their fortune. How many wild lands around this world were first tamed by folk like us? How many foreign wars were fought for Britain by Highland armies? They will go, the young ones—I know it."

Many of the older ones nodded sadly. And perhaps some of them, too, felt a stir within themselves—a kindling of an ancient wanderlust in their blood, that hardy adventurousness which had once placed Highlanders on every dangerous frontier around the world.

Tears were dimming the eyes of Donal's mother

as she turned to Cord. "Nor do I blame you, Cord. You do what you must. But I do not thank you. For if you take Donal on this journey, you take him from me forever."

"Perhaps not," Samella said softly. "If the rebellion succeeds, the free colonies will keep many links with Earth. People may be able to travel back and forth before long. You would see your son again."

As the mother brightened, Donal slapped Cord heavily on the shoulder. "Until yesterday," he cried, "I thought the great adventure of my life would be to travel to the city. And now—you're to take me to the stars!"

"Then you'll join us?" Samella asked.

"I will," Donal said. "And so will most of us here. Then tomorrow we'll carry the word to others. Cord, I expect to have three or four dozen of us waiting for your spaceship when it returns."

"You'll not need many others, Cord," joked another youth. "One Highlander in a fight would be worth ten of those starvelings from the cities that you speak of."

Cord laughed. "Once I would have said the same, Jamie. But wait till you've met them and fought beside them, as I have."

From there the talk shifted to practicalities, about seeking other young people from surrounding villages and farms, and the place where they were to await Lathan's ship. And slowly the mood of the gathering changed. It became less like a meeting and more like a party—to welcome Cord and to celebrate the prospect of adventure. Bottles appeared as if by magic, and everyone laughed good-naturedly as Samella spluttered over her first taste of malt whisky. Soon the pipes and other instruments raised their voices, and the folk were spilling out of the overcrowded cottage, building a great fire in the open air, leaping like demons in their athletic dances while the blood-stirring music filled the gathering dusk.

"Barbarians," Samella muttered to Cord with a grin. He laughed, and swung her into the throes of another dance.

The celebration went on through the night. But it was also tinged with sorrow, for in part it was a farewell. So sometimes the dancing stopped and the music of the pipes arched upwards in a sonorous lament. But then the drinking and feasting and dancing would resume, until at last the dawn revealed the ashes of the fire's remains, and the revellers stumbled away to snore by their hearths.

By the next evening, when Donal and the others had returned from beginning to spread the word, it was time for Cord and Samella to take their leave. Once again they grew chilled and wet as they walked, though they felt more discomfort from pounding headaches. But they felt satisfaction as well. The job had been done—warriors had been recruited for the Klydor army.

If only it could be so easy, Cord thought, when we get to Limbo.

*　　　*　　　*

Within a few hours they were back aboard the ship. Lathan had already picked up Heleth and the two Streeters, whose efforts in the Bunkers had also been successful. Now Lathan was to deliver the five of them to a spot near the metropolis that contained Limbo. He would then go back into orbit, to wait while the groups of young warriors from the High- lands and the Bunkers gathered at the assembly points. Lathan was to ferry them out to the rebel base in the Asteroid Belt, while Cord and his friends made their way to Limbo.

"Lots of Vampires coming," Heleth announced happily as the ship rose into the night. "Near a hundred, maybe. The Bunkers are getting a little crowded, and some of the troop feel restless."

"Not all," Rontal said. "One fell' figured she was makin' it all up—called her a liar."

"She bashed him fine," Jeko said, laughing.

Heleth shrugged. "I've had trouble with that yeck-head before. He's nothing. But having these two along"—she gestured at Rontal and Jeko—"helped. Everyone worked out that the only way two Streeters could get to the Bunkers was the way I told them."

Jeko grimaced. "Wasn't much fun, though. Talk about *creepy*. One minute you're in an empty tunnel, all cold slimy rock, can't see a thing, and you reckon there's nobody for miles. Next minute, you're in a crowd. You can't see 'em, but you *know* they're there, watchin'. Like—like dead folk, comin' up from graves."

Heleth snorted. "You're just as creepy to them, yeck-mouth. Creepier."

Rontal intervened before Jeko could reply. "One thing that got them goin' was when Heleth told 'em about the caves on Klydor, where we were before. She said once we got ColSec sorted out, they could all live there."

Lathan nodded. "If we get ColSec sorted out, the Bunker people can live anywhere they want."

By then the ship was outside the atmosphere, in a low orbit, while Lathan prepared to land in the American Segment. And tension silenced the teenagers as the ship finally began to curve downwards.

"All clear below," Lathan said, watching the scanner screens. "We're landing in a patch of wasteland, with scrubby woods around it, near the edge of the city. No sign of life near those woods, and it's a cloudy night."

"You're gonna like this city," Jeko said to Cord. "And with me and Rontal showin' the way, everything's gonna be fine. This recruitin' is easy—like all the CeeDees are asleep."

A chill fled along Cord's spine as he heard those fate-tempting words. But he brushed the feeling aside, watching the viewport as the ship plunged down through the clouds.

"Let me tell it one more time," Lathan said. "You bring your Streeters out to the place where we'll land *three nights* from now—seventy-two hours. I'll watch for you on the scanners." He smiled faintly. "Try not to get...held up. You're going to be needed, back on Klydor."

The others nodded silently. As they stared out

at the surface of the Earth hurtling up to meet them, each of them seemed to be thinking the same thought that was churning through Cord's mind.

I wonder, they thought, *if we'll ever see Klydor again.*

6

The Metropolis

The five friends crouched within a stand of scrub pine, surrounded by the humid warmth of a summer night. A few minutes before, they had watched the flare of the spaceship vanish in the heaviness of cloud above them. Now they waited, silently, in case someone brave enough—or official enough—came to find out what was going on in that dark stretch of woods.

But after many long minutes, Heleth straightened. "No one's around," she said. "Just little animals in the bushes."

The others stood up, knowing that Heleth's hearing was as remarkable as her night vision. "Got away with it again," Jeko said with a snicker.

Once more that flash of cold sped along Cord's spine—a superstitious dread of claiming success before it has been achieved. "We haven't got to the hard part yet," he said sharply.

They moved out of the woods, flitting like shadows across an empty field. In the distance, the night sky seemed to be glowing, as if a vast fire was burning. Cord knew that he was seeing the reflected lights of the gigantic city. They would have to make their way through that city, through all its vast networks of streets, its enormous population—and its contingents of Civil Defenders. The chill spread again along his nerves, like an electric shock. But he clenched his teeth and strode on.

"Funny," Rontal said quietly. "I never been out here before, beyond the city. 'Cept when the CeeDees had me, but then I never saw much of anythin' till I woke up on Klydor."

"Same here," Jeko murmured. "We could *be* on Klydor, for all I know." He gestured at the glow in the sky. "But at least we know which way to go."

It took more than an hour, of skulking through wasteland and farmland, for them to reach the city's fringe. There they found small shabby buildings on rough and narrow streets—which were also badly lit, to their relief. The buildings looked like rows of identical boxes, four storeys high, all the same dull brown.

"Workers' places," Rontal whispered. "Poor folk, down at the bottom of things, crowded out here 'cause there's nowhere else."

No lights showed in any of the narrow windows, and no person—except the five teenagers—stirred on the streets. But Cord had expected that. According to the two Streeters, the Organization imposed a curfew on the metropolis. People had to have good official reasons, and passes, to be out of their homes— legally—at night.

The rows of four-storey boxes seemed to be endless, until at last Jeko and Rontal found a slightly broader street leading to a different district. The buildings were still identical boxes, but much taller, with more windows and even patches of dry grass around them. Unfortunately, that district also had better street lighting, and the five had to skirt nervously around the pools of light, edging along the sides of the buildings.

Another series of deserted streets led them to an area of seedy-looking shops, interspersed with grimy industrial buildings. And there they had to leap for a shadowy alley between two shops, hearts pounding, when they heard the distant murmur of a powerful engine.

"Sounds like a floater patrol," Jeko muttered.

Cord then learned that a floater was a vehicle that hovered on a cushion of air, smaller and faster than the CeeDee hovertanks, but well-armed and armoured. The information did not improve his state of mind—for the sound of the engine was growing closer.

They fled along the narrow alley, led through its darkness by Heleth. Its sides were thickly littered with garbage and human waste, producing foul odours as heavy as poison gas. Briefly their way was barred by a wire-mesh fence, but one end sagged limply so they could squeeze through. Beyond it they crouched in deep blackness among a stack of reeking metal containers.

The thrumming of the floater drew even closer. They shrank back, nerves jangling.

"Comin' straight this way," Jeko hissed. "Maybe after us."

"Do you think we were spotted?" Samella asked. "Or set off some alarm?"

"No way of knowin'," Rontal replied. "I thought we been clear, but..."

He broke off. The floater's rumble had now become a throaty roar, as the vehicle entered the street beyond the alley where they crouched. Cord inched forward, glimpsing the floater's lights at the mouth of the alley. Then he jerked back, just in time. The wall next to him was suddenly bathed in brilliance, as the floater's spotlights blazed into the alley.

But the blast of brightness ended almost as it began. The alley was plunged back into darkness as the spotlight withdrew. The floater's engine changed pitch, then slowly began to fade. In moments the sound was only a receding murmur again, as the vehicle sped away.

The teenagers let out their breath in shaky sighs. "Just a patrol," Rontal said.

"Just *one* patrol," Jeko said ominously. "There'll be more."

"Hope they keep their lights to themselves," Heleth grumbled. "That spotlight *hurt.*"

When she had recovered her night vision, they continued their progress. A further hour passed, with only one brief alarm, when the throb of another distant floater was picked up by Heleth's alert ears. But that one came nowhere near them. And by then they had passed through many different districts—especially more residential estates, with more of the unappealing box-like buildings, and a few more of the areas that mixed small businesses with shabby light industry.

But beyond them, a wider street led into a sector of substantial houses and apartment blocks, much better kept, with lush greenery around them.

"Richer part of town," Rontal said. "Important folk live here. An' if we go through, it's a shorter way to the centre, to Limbo. But there's a problem."

"We could do with a shortcut," Cord said.

"Sure," Jeko said. "But rich areas have lotsa lights, and more CeeDee patrols—along with private security, dogs, alarms..."

"Then we stay out," Samella said quickly. "It isn't worth the risk."

"Which makes another problem," Rontal said. "Quickest way round this area takes us into the territory of another troop. A small bunch, but they think they're hard. Call themselves the Hatchet-men. They see us, we're in trouble."

"If *anybody* sees us, we're in trouble," Heleth growled.

Rontal nodded. "I'd as soon run into Hatchetmen as CeeDees. And if we go that way, we might find a place to hide if we can't get to Limbo 'fore daylight."

"We'd lose a whole day," Cord said unhappily.

"Worse things we could lose," Jeko said.

So they decided to skirt round the dangerous area of wealthier houses and to risk entering the territory of the smaller gang, the Hatchetmen, hoping to sneak through safely and make it to Limbo before sunrise.

They angled away, following the two Streeters through a succession of slightly broader and more respectable roadways. For one startling moment, they found themselves on the crest of a rise—and through a gap among the buildings, they glimpsed magnificence in the distance. Ranks of mighty skyscrapers, rearing like a mountain range into the night sky, gleaming with lights that revealed the clean lines of the structures, the spires at their breathtaking summits.

"New city centre," Rontal said briefly. "Old centre's not too far from it." He pointed to a broad sweep of darkness, looking flat and empty compared to the grandeur of the towers. "That's Limbo."

Cord nodded. It didn't seem too far, he thought. If they hurried, they could make it before first light. And there didn't seem to be anything to slow them down.

Shortly they entered another poor, older section, with narrow grubby streets and many different kinds of buildings, all jammed together and in a miserable state of disrepair. The buildings seemed to be leaning shakily against each other for support, and most of the windows were boarded up, like the blank sockets of blind eyes. The streets were awash with litter, many of them half-choked with heaps of rubble and junk. And many buildings were wholly derelict, where roofs had collapsed or where fire had left only blackened skeletons of brick and concrete.

Jeko grinned at the look on Cord's face. "Limbo looks like this," he said. "Only more of it—and worse."

But then they were silenced by an abrupt jerk of Heleth's hand. "Don't talk!" she snapped. "I heard something!"

They halted, straining their ears. But the dismal street and the wretched buildings remained silent and still. It seemed almost a menacing stillness, as if every blank window and every heap of crumbled concrete sheltered enemies, lying in wait. Nerves afire with tension, the five crept forward.

At the next corner, where a jagged metal stump was all that remained of a streetlight, they paused again. No light at all seemed to reach into the blackness of the street to their left—and not the slightest whisper of sound emerged from that blackness. Yet some instinct sent a wave of iciness along Cord's back, lifting the hairs on his neck.

The two Streeters edged soundlessly forward, taking a few steps around the corner, into the tomblike blackness of that side street. Cord and Samella hung back for a moment, looking at Heleth. As far as Cord could tell in the darkness, Heleth had closed her eyes, to focus her hearing. Cord touched her arm, to indicate that they should follow the others.

But before they could move, the blackness of the side street vanished in an eruption of light.

The stark white glare swept over them like a shock wave. Cord's half-yell of surprise and fear mingled with a cry from Samella—and a shriek of pain from Heleth, as the blast of light struck at her vision even through her closed eyelids. The two Streeters, several steps away, stood transfixed in the glare, like moths in a flame. Then Cord's heart seemed to stop as horror grasped him.

Behind that explosion of light he had glimpsed a mighty bulk. A bulk that lifted itself slightly from the ground, enveloped at once in a cloud of dust and grit.

Engine thundering at full throttle, the CeeDee hovertank surged towards them.

7

First Ambush

Half-dazed with the shock of glimpsing the terror-machine, Cord saw the two Streeters wheel and leap back towards him. Jeko's mouth opened, shouting something that was drowned by the hideous bellow of the hovertank. Samella, white-faced, was supporting the sagging body of Heleth, whose eyes were squeezed shut with pain.

The daze lifted from Cord like a blanket being flung aside. Rontal and Jeko sprinted past, waving arms to urge the others on. Cord reached for Heleth, flung her over one broad shoulder, and leaped after the Streeters, Samella beside him.

Heleth's sturdy body seemed weightless as adrenaline flowed through Cord's powerful muscles. In a few strides he and Samella were on the Streeters' heels, hurtling back the way they had come in a headlong

51

dash. None of them could see properly, after that lightblast from the hovertank, but they did not slow their pace. Stumbling over the broken, cluttered pavement, they slipped and tripped and caught their balance and raced on. It was a desperate flight made out of overwhelming terror, like five small animals fleeing in panic from a monstrous predator.

Behind them, the hovertank roared around the corner. The blaze of light reached the length of the street, picking them out in their frantic dash.

But their flight was not entirely hysterical, for all its fear-filled pace. And it was Samella who spotted the open doorway, with its broken door hanging askew.

"In there!" she shrieked.

Instantly the group veered to one side. Jeko even had time to flash a look of appreciation at Samella, before they plunged into the darkness of the building's interior. Their pace did not slacken as they leaped across sagging floorboards, crashing painfully into unseen obstacles. Something caught at Cord's foot and he nearly fell full-length before finding his balance. Yet still Heleth seemed weightless on his shoulder as he hurled himself after the others, towards another gaping doorway, bursting out into a damp and reeking passage that was the mirror image of the alley they had been in earlier.

"Alley's too narrow for the tank!" Jeko yelled.

"It'll just smash through!" Rontal replied. "Keep goin'!"

They sprinted away, the far end of the alley

looming dimly. Behind them, they heard the thunder of the hovertank deepen, and with it heard the appalling sound of a building being suddenly demolished. Wood splintered like gunfire, concrete boomed as it was flung aside in an avalanche of rubble. The CeeDee hovertank crashed through the derelict building like a bull through a paper hoop.

They fled across a narrow street and into another passage between crumbling buildings. At one side a barely visible doorway appeared—and the door exploded open under a ferocious leaping kick from Rontal. Then they were stumbling through that building, bouncing off more walls and other obstacles, hardly aware of bruised flesh and cracked shins. It was a sizeable building, perhaps once a warehouse—but they were across it in seconds, leaping out of another door, flashing across another empty street.

The chase went on and on, streets and alleys, darkened doorways and cluttered interiors. Yet the headlong speed of their flight did not lessen. And behind them, the bellow of the hovertank began to recede slightly, as if some of their twists and turns had confused the pursuers. We're losing them, Cord thought elatedly—and the thought seemed to lend more strength to his legs.

Many minutes later, many more stinking alleys and rubble-strewn buildings farther, they began to slow their pace. The sound of the hovertank had faded to a distant growl and seemed to be dying away completely.

"Reckon we lost 'em," Rontal said, as they halted at last, gasping for breath.

"Like old times," Jeko exulted. "CeeDees crashin' around with tanks and lights, Streeters disappearin' every which way like puffs of smoke. Takes more'n *one* hovertank to catch Streeters, in territory like this."

"But it's not Limbo," Rontal said tersely. "We're off our route an' we've lost a lotta time. An' we're in the middle of Hatchetmen land. Lucky we didn't run into some, in those buildin's."

"How's Heleth?" Jeko asked. And Cord was almost surprised to find that she was still draped limply over his shoulder. As he began to lower her, she stirred and moaned.

"That light really hurt her," Samella murmured. "She fainted..."

"She's coming round," Cord said. In the dimness they could see her eyelids flutter. Then her eyes snapped open, like two huge pools of glistening darkness.

"Cord..." she said. "It's you!"

"Who else?" Cord said with a smile.

"I mean I can see you!" Heleth said. She found her balance and stepped back, staring around. "I can *see*!" The tears in her tormented eyes spilled over, wetness shining on her blackened cheeks.

"Heleth, don't," Samella said gently. "We're all right, and the hovertank is gone."

"Thought I was blinded," Heleth muttered. "That light hurt so much—like my eyes caught fire."

"Lucky you didn't get the full blast," Rontal said. "You an' Cord an' Samella stayed back a bit, remember?"

Heleth nodded. "And I had my eyes closed." She shuddered, remembering.

Jeko nudged her sturdy shoulder. "Glad you did," he said. "Now you can get back to findin' the way through all this dark. While you were havin' a nice sleep on Cord's shoulder, we were crashin' through all kind of junk. Runnin'... blind."

Only then was Cord aware of the various messages of pain from bruised shoulders and shins and elbows and knees, which had collided with solid objects in all the darkened ways they had taken during their flight.

Heleth scowled. "I got some bruises, too. Like Cord was using me as a shield, a lot of the time."

"Couldn't help it..." Cord began lamely—but halted. Heleth had stiffened, as her gaze shifted.

"You won't be needing my eyes for a while," she said in a low voice. "Look up."

They looked, and Cord's heart sank. Above the rotting roofs, one part of the sky showed streaks of grey, faint but unmistakeable.

Day was breaking over the city.

"We got a while yet," Rontal said as they moved swiftly away. "Curfew ends at sunrise, not first light."

"But we gotta find a place," Jeko said. "Somewhere to stay hid, all day. And in the middle of Hatchetmen territory."

"And the CeeDees will be looking for us," Samella said sombrely. "They'll put out a major alert."

"Maybe not," Rontal replied, to their surprise. "Samella, you an' Cord an' Heleth were hangin' back. CeeDees saw Jeko an' me clear enough, but maybe not you."

"Right!" Jeko said hopefully. "They coulda just thought you were three more Streeters, and not looked too close. They chased us, lost us and went on their way. Nothin' new—they're chasin' Streeters nearly every night. They won't have a big alert over that."

"If they were," Rontal added, "we'd know by now. The streets'd be crawlin' with tanks an' floaters, an' flyers overhead. I reckon we're okay—if we can find a hideout."

As they moved on, Cord felt sure that Rontal was right. If the CeeDees had spotted the three outsiders—especially Heleth, with her unmistakeable face—they would certainly have been highly suspicious, and would have launched a search of the area in force. But a few wandering Streeters, breaking the curfew—as Jeko said, there was nothing unusual about that.

So they pressed on, through streets that remained as empty and silent as in the middle of the night. The ordinary people of the city were not yet stirring, in the dawn, and no CeeDee vehicles could be heard in the vicinity. But even so, they could not relax. The need for a place to hide during the daylight hours would soon grow desperate. And there was still the threat of the other gang, the Hatchetmen, who could be lurking anywhere in that desolate area.

Not until half an hour later, when the sky was showing the first glints of a red and orange sunrise, did they find the hideaway they needed. Another foul alley had led them into a kind of courtyard—a sheltered area surrounded on three sides by the blank concrete walls of buildings. The courtyard held a number of long, low sheds, looking unused, with empty window frames and sagging roofs. They offered seclusion, well away from any street, and were unlikely to attract interest except from the rats that scuttled along the alleys.

"Won't do better'n that," Rontal whispered. "Let's check 'em out."

"Me first," Heleth said. She was entirely recovered now, and her habitual scowl settled on her brow as she moved silently towards the door of the nearest shed, the others crowding behind her. Cord heard the faint rasps as Heleth and the two Streeters slid their blades from their sheaths.

"Lots of junk in here," Heleth whispered from the doorway. "Dumped all over the place."

"Makes it better, for hidin'," Rontal said softly.

Heleth stepped forward, vanishing into the darkness of the interior. The others followed, and for a moment Cord wished that the sun was already fully up, shedding some light into the place. He was heartily sick of darkness and foul smells and the filthy, cluttered interiors of run-down buildings. He grew even sicker when he struck an already bruised shin against some hard unseen object, and only just managed to swallow the grunt of pain.

In that moment, from the darkness ahead, he heard a fierce hiss—like the noise Jeko made when he was agitated. Then faint scuffling noises arose all around. He stiffened, trying hard to see through the blackness.

The next sounds occurred all at once. Several heavy thuds, a grunt, a muffled snarl, and a yelp of pain.

And before Cord could move, a heavy body landed squarely on his back and bore him crashing to the floor.

8

Stele

An athlete's reflexes and sheer muscular power kept Cord's arms solidly braced, despite the weight on his back, as his hands struck the floor. Then he reached back one-handed over his shoulder, clutched a handful of cloth and jerked forward. The weight vanished from his back as the attacker flew over his shoulder, crashing to the floor with an explosive gasp.

But Cord had not released his grip. Grasping more of his attacker's clothing with his other hand, he surged smoothly to his feet. And with a mighty heave, he simply flung the attacker away into the darkness.

A loud crash and a shriek of pain told him that the attacker had not landed comfortably. He groped through the darkness, towards the other cries and crashes where his friends were being attacked. But before he reached them, a voice rang out—clear and crisp, with a note of command.

"Hold it! Back off! We're fighting *Streeters*!"

"This's no Streeter," snarled a different voice, elsewhere in the blackness. But then the shadows were banished, by a number of small lights held aloft in several hands.

Cord stared around wildly. Jeko and Rontal stood, knives in hand, against one wall where they had been grappling with several dark forms. Near them Samella was pinned to a stack of crates by a pair of attackers, and three more were piled on to Heleth on the floor. Part of Cord's mind told him that the second strange voice had come from that last group. But most of his mind was dealing with the shock of seeing the attackers.

There were about twenty of them, young people wearing sleeveless leather shirts, tight dark trousers and high boots. And every one of them had smooth hairless heads, with ridged scars forming letters, and a silvery "s" embedded in their foreheads.

"Streeters!" Cord blurted.

Jeko straightened, smiling fiercely, his eyes locked on one of the strange Streeters in front of him. A tall, pale youth, hard-muscled and wiry, who seemed to be in command—the one, Cord guessed, who had stopped the attack.

The pale youth returned Jeko's stare blankly. "Jeko and Rontal," he breathed. "What part of hell did they send you back from?"

"Nice to see you, Stele," Jeko said. "You givin' this party just for us?"

"Don't stop it if you don't wanta," Rontal drawled. "Was just gettin' to be fun."

Jeko snickered. And then the shed was suddenly filled with laughter and excited voices. The other Streeters crowded around Jeko and Rontal, sometimes prodding or punching them lightly as if to be sure they were real. Then the pale youth called Stele held up a sinewy hand and the noise died away, as the crowd turned to face Cord and the two girls who were standing together to one side.

"We thought you were Hatchetmen," Stele said. He half-turned towards Rontal, but did not take his eyes from the three strangers.

"We thought *you* were," Rontal replied. "What you doin' here, outa Limbo?"

Stele shrugged. "That'll keep. What matters is what you're doing here—with these."

Jeko's eyes glinted. "*These* are our friends. And we're on our way to Limbo to tell the Streeters a story that'll shake you enough to make your hair grow back."

That drew smiles and a murmur of curiosity from the crowd, silenced as Stele spoke again.

"Nothing like a good story," he said. "Maybe you should tell some of it now. Strangers don't get much of a welcome in Limbo—you know that, Jeko."

"We haven't had much of a welcome so far," Cord said heatedly.

The pale youth studied him. "So it talks," he said sardonically.

"That ain't all it does," said a voice from the crowd. "Threw me around like I didn't weigh nothin'."

That drew a laugh, for the speaker was squat and hefty—and obviously was the one who had jumped on Cord. Then Cord looked more closely and realized that the hairless head had misled him. His attacker was a girl—as were several of the others, including the pair who had overcome Samella.

"That one's Cord," Rontal was saying. "He comes from a buncha wild folk in the Highlands, north Britain. He's kinda strong, with a short temper." That raised another laugh and some curious stares aimed at Cord. "The blonde is Samella, used to be an indent over in Minneap'. She's prob'ly smarter'n the rest of you put together." That drew further stares. "An' the third one is Heleth, from the Vampires troop in the Bunkers under Old London. She can see in the dark like a cat."

"Didn't do her much good here," someone said mockingly.

"You were hiding in all this junk, yeck-mouth!" Heleth flared. "You want to try again?"

More laughter rose, and Cord had to take a firm hold on Heleth's shirt to keep her from charging at the entire crowd. Then Stele's voice brought silence once more.

"You really from those places?" he asked.

"Yes," Cord said shortly.

"And like Jeko said," Samella put in, "we've

come to talk to the Streeters. Not to look for trouble."

"But you can have trouble if you want it," Heleth snarled.

Stele smiled faintly, then turned to Jeko. "You said you had a story to tell. We've got all day to hear it, because we can't move from here till dark. So go ahead. And don't forget to tell where you two have been all this time."

Jeko grinned. "That's the story—where we been. We got lifted by CeeDees, got sent a *long* way away, got ourselves back. That's the bare bones of it. Only it gets interestin' when we tell you *where* we were sent." He looked around at his audience, enjoying the drama of the moment. "We got sent into *space*. To another planet. But it's *our* planet now—and we've come back to offer the Streeters a share in it."

Jeko was an excellent storyteller. He relished being in centre stage and knew exactly how to hold the attention of his audience, making the images and dramas of Klydor come alive in their minds. The Streeters were enthralled. Many of them also seemed excited by the idea of a rebellion and of fighting on a faraway planet.

Sensibly—and with the help of a warning look from Samella—Jeko did not go into the details of how recruits were to be taken from Earth. He merely gave his listeners a general idea of the rebel demands that would be put before ColSec, then wound up his story. A general hubbub arose, mingling jokes and comments and questions, but it faded as before when Stele raised a hand.

"Good stuff," he said to Jeko. "It'd make a great vid series."

"You get the Organization to pay for it," Jeko said with a grin, "I'll star in it."

Stele smiled briefly. "Let's boil it down," he said. "You're here to raise a little army from the Streeters and other troops. It's going to be taken to this planet, Klydor, to protect it if ColSec attacks."

"Some of it's prob'ly on its way now," Rontal said.

"Okay," Stele went on. "Now suppose everything goes right for the rebels. ColSec says, you win, all the planets can be free. What happens then to all the folk who've gone to Klydor in your army?"

Jeko looked taken aback by Stele's clear mind going straight to a very crucial point. But Samella filled the gap.

"If we win," she said, "the people on Klydor can stay there if they want to. It's a big world."

"What if some didn't want to?" Stele asked.

Samella smiled. "We're fighting for *freedom*. Anyone will be free to go where they want. Maybe some would find life on Klydor too much like hard work"—that raised some dry laughter—"so they could go to one of the older, established colony worlds if they wanted to. Or maybe some would want to come back to the peaceful joys and beauties of this city." The Streeters laughed again, as her gesture indicated the cluttered, filthy interior of the shed. "So they could be brought back just as we were brought here."

Stele nodded, looking thoughtful, and a brief silence fell, broken at last by the hefty girl who had attacked Cord.

"Dunno why you're talkin' about what happens *after*," she complained. "I'm still tryin' to get used to the whole idea of other planets an' stuff."

"We know it's not easy to take in all at once," Samella said. "But it's true. And we'll answer any questions you have."

"Our questions don't matter too much," Stele said wryly. "It's Tuller you have to convince."

"Tuller's chief of the Streeters," Jeko explained, in response to Cord's inquiring look.

"Chief?" Cord said, surprised. "I thought Stele was."

Stele shook his head. "I'm just a general—I get to organize some of the action that we start, like last night. Tuller's been chief a long time."

"What were you doin' last night?" Rontal asked.

"Looking for Hatchetmen," Stele said. "They've been getting pushy, raiding stores for supplies near Limbo, things like that. We came to remind them who's who. Only we didn't find any of them, and we're stuck here for the day."

Again Jeko and Rontal explained to the other three. Once the Streeters had been the only outlaw gang in the metropolis, since they controlled Limbo, which offered a haven that kept them more or less safe from the CeeDees. But more recently, as other parts of the city had deteriorated, a few smaller gangs had grown up in those sections—like the Hatchetmen.

They were a weird troop, Jeko added, bleaching their hair stark white and painting their faces blood-red. And they could be fairly dangerous with their favourite weapons which were, as their name implied, nasty little hand-axes.

"How many Hatchetmen these days?" Rontal asked.

"Not many," Stele said. "Forty, forty-five."

Samella's eyebrows rose. "And twenty of you were going to take them on?"

"Twenty *Streeters*, chuck," Stele said with a grin. "More than enough." His grin took on an edge of challenge. "'Course, if we run into them tonight, we *could* be twenty-five."

It was Cord's turn to raise his eyebrows. "Are you asking us to join in this fight?"

Stele's dark eyes hardened. "You want us to join *your* fight, fell'," he said coolly. "It'd do you a lot of good if Tuller hears that you joined ours."

"We're in," Jeko said at once.

"Wouldn't miss it," Rontal added.

Cord glanced at Samella, concern for her safety showing in his eyes, and found that she was looking at him with an expression that was both defiant and determined. "I'm not..." he began uneasily.

Samella cut in. "We'll join you," she said flatly. "If we have to prove ourselves."

"Good," Stele said, smiling as he noted Cord's troubled expression. "Now we can take it easy, till night. We've got food and stuff for you. And you can tell us some more stories about these other planets." He clapped Cord on the shoulder. "Don't look so worried, fell'. The Hatchetmen only have *little* axes. They'll be no trouble—compared to what might happen when you meet Tuller."

9

Second Ambush

Night finally returned to the metropolis, to the relief of everyone in that crowded shed. The day had been far hotter and more humid than the previous night, and twenty-five sweating teenagers had turned the shed into a place that could rival even the most foul alley. But the darkness brought a drop in temperature, which lifted everyone's spirits.

"Trouble is," Stele said as they prepared to leave the shed, "the Hatchetmen may stay out of our way. If we don't find them tonight, we'll have to head back to Limbo and try another time."

That idea pleased Cord—because of Samella. He knew she was brave, as well as being skilled with many high-tech weapons. But here she was unarmed—and, being slim and slight, she was no gang warrior.

Anyway, Cord told himself, we have a job to do, and shouldn't be getting into pointless street fights.

His troubled thoughts cut off. Heleth had naturally been one of the first out of the shed, into the darkened courtyard beyond. Cord saw her halt abruptly, head cocked, then turn to Stele.

"We got a problem," she growled. "We're surrounded."

Stele's teeth flashed in a fierce grin. "Hatchetmen," he murmured.

Cord grasped Samella's arm. "Stay in the shed till this is over."

But to his astonishment she turned on him, eyes blazing. "I don't need that," she snapped. "I survived on the northern plains and in the streets of Minneapolis. I've looked after myself for years, Cord MaKiy, without your help—and I'll look after myself tonight."

And before Cord could find any words to argue with her, it was too late.

A chilling yell arose from the darkness. And forty-five wild-looking youths poured into the courtyard at a run.

They looked like demons, Cord thought. The dim glow of a distant streetlight illuminated their spiky white hair, their scarlet faces, and the razor edges of the hand-axes that they brandished. They wore high-necked tunics and trousers, with crimson axe-symbols painted on their chests. But there was no time to study them further, or for Cord to find a weapon. The Streeters were fanning out to meet the charge.

Cord glanced around and saw, to his horror, that

Samella had disappeared, lost elsewhere in the shadows. But he could not search for her—because two Hatchetmen were bearing down on him, evil grins on their demonic faces.

Sudden battle-rage flared within Cord, born mostly out of his fear for Samella. The two attackers seemed to be approaching in slow motion, so as the first one leaped forward Cord seemed to have plenty of time to dodge aside, and to strike with all his speed and power. His fist crashed into the first attacker's face, and the Hatchetman staggered back, impeding his partner. In that instant Cord swung again, a furious blow that brought the sodden crunch of breaking bone. The second Hatchetman stumbled and fell, his nose smashed, the red mask of his face no longer wholly due to paint.

But Cord's feet were suddenly swept from under him. As he landed heavily on his back, his head thumped on to the concrete, and his vision filled with flashing lights. Through a blur he dimly saw that the first Hatchetman had recovered. His axe gleamed evilly as he raised it over Cord's fallen body.

Numbly, Cord tried to roll aside. But the blow to his head had briefly short-circuited his nerves. He could only stare upwards through his daze, as the axe reached the top of its swing.

Then a lithe and shadowy shape hurled itself like a projectile against the Hatchetman. The impact sent the axe-wielder lurching forward, sprawling when his foot slipped on a broken patch of concrete. But he bounced to his feet with frightening speed, facing his new enemy.

With another surge of horror, Cord saw that it was Samella who had saved him. Now she faced the Hatchetman, bare-handed, looking absurdly small. The sight dragged Cord out of his daze, and he fought to regain his feet.

The Hatchetman gave a hoarse bellow and sprang at Samella, axe flashing up.

"No!" Cord yelled, lunging forward.

But there was no need. Samella took a step away and snatched up a handful of dusty earth from the patch of broken concrete, flinging it full in the Hatchetman's face. Half-blinded, the axe-wielder halted, pawing at his eyes.

And with cold ferocity and all the strength she could muster, Samella kicked him squarely between the legs.

Eyes bulging nearly out of their sockets, the Hatchetman squealed like an injured pig, and folded in the middle as if his backbone had been removed.

Samella shot Cord a look of pure triumph. "*Now* who needs looking after?" she yelled.

Cord grinned. But his expression changed as he looked past her. The mêlée of the fight had moved away from them, leaving a scattering of fallen bodies—most with blood-red faces. But to one side, Stele had his back to a wall, a heavy knife in his hand, confronting three of the enemy.

"*He* does!" Cord shouted, and raced away.

As he ran, the Hatchetmen closed in on Stele

but were driven back by the skilled sweep of his blade. Then Cord arrived. Two of the enemy became aware of him at the last minute and began to whirl towards him. For a fraction of a second, as they turned, they faced each other.

In that micro-instant Cord reached out, clutched two handsful of spiky white hair and slammed their heads together with all his remarkable strength.

The two scarlet foreheads collided with a grisly crunch—which was followed at once by another. The third attacker had leaped at Stele, axe slashing. But Stele neatly dodged the blow, clamped the enemy's arm, and ran him face first into the concrete wall.

Grinning, Stele turned to Cord. But then they froze. A new noise had risen above the clatter and shouts of battle. A distant thrumming roar, which Cord now knew very well.

"Break off! CeeDees!"

The cry came from Stele, clear and commanding. And the fighting ended as if rehearsed. The combatants parted, and the few Hatchetmen who were still standing melted away into the darkness.

"Streeters, pick up the wounded and move!" Stele yelled.

Again the movements seemed rehearsed. Among the fallen Hatchetmen—about two-thirds of their force, Cord guessed—were the sprawled forms of six or eight Streeters. Two of those were left where they were, since they were past all aid. But the others were gathered up, and the Streeters also vanished into the night.

Cord blinked to find that Stele also had disappeared. Then a jaunty voice spoke from behind him.

"Stele always gets the wounded home," it said. Cord turned to see Jeko and Rontal, unharmed, grinning at him. Samella joined them, with Heleth, who was nursing a superficial slash along one arm.

"Now we run again!" Jeko said.

They fled from the courtyard like wraiths, led by the two Streeters and guided again by Heleth's night vision. As they sped through another series of narrow streets, the sound of the CeeDee vehicles slowly dwindled behind them. Soon they felt safe enough to pause for breath, and again Jeko was laughing.

"CeeDees'll be pickin' up Hatchetmen," he said. "So maybe soon ColSec'll be throwin' *them* out into space, to some wild planet."

"Not if the rebellion succeeds," Samella said firmly.

"It'd serve them right, even so," Heleth growled.

"Like it did us?" Rontal asked.

And their muffled laughter eased their tension as they resumed their stealthy flight towards Limbo.

The next two hours, as they raced through the unappealing streets, proved uneventful. Jeko and Rontal then announced that they had crossed the "border" into Limbo—though to Cord the streets around them looked no more or less decrepit and filthy than the previous ones. About half an hour later, they were suddenly surrounded by Streeters, emerging from half-ruined buildings around them, led by a grinning Stele.

"I hoped you'd make it," he said, looking especially at Cord. "I owe you for what you did back there."

Cord smiled wryly. "If you feel that way, put in a good word for us with your chief, Tuller."

"Tuller took a group to get supplies," Stele said. "Won't be back till morning, so you can relax for a while. Some of the troop will get you some food and show you where you can sleep. And I'll have a word with Tuller, first thing."

"Shouldn't we be there?" Samella asked.

Stele shook his head. "Better not. I'll tell him your story—and about tonight—and you can fill in details, after." His eyes narrowed. "Let me give you some advice. Tuller's hard and mean, and getting meaner this past year or so. But he's the *chief*. He expects respect and obedience, and he gets it. The Streeters feel friendly towards you now, but you're still strangers—and they'd chop you up tomorrow if Tuller told them to. So watch what you say to him, and how you say it."

Cord looked at him levelly. "Would *you* help to chop us up, if Tuller says?"

Stele grinned. "We'll have to see, won't we? Just hope it doesn't come to that."

Cord awoke with a start out of some shapeless dream of menace. The five of them had slept on reasonably clean mattresses, in a cool cellar. Now the morning light was filtering through the wooden planks of the cellar's ceiling—which was all that remained of the building above. Cord had felt that, while they were not prisoners, they were also not quite honoured guests. The Streeters had treated them well, but were clearly waiting for their chief's orders before they made the newcomers fully welcome—or otherwise.

But those feelings had not kept Cord and the others from sleeping deeply, after the stresses and battles of the previous night. As Cord awoke, two Streeters entered, carrying bowls of something that smelled wonderful. The five of them perched on their mattresses, enjoying the food and the rare moment of peace. It was the first time that Cord had felt relaxed since their arrival in the American Segment, and he was savouring the absence of tension as much as the food.

Then Stele walked into the cellar. And with him came a renewal of tension, and perhaps something worse.

Stele threw Cord a look that seemed to mingle a warning with a hint of apology. The towering figure next to him had no expression at all on his heavy features. He seemed to be in his late twenties, or even older, powerfully built, with close-set eyes that stared silently at the newcomers.

"This is Tuller," Stele said flatly.

Cord and the others rose slowly, returning Tuller's blank-eyed scrutiny.

"Stele's been tellin' me some stories," Tuller said

at last, in a hoarse voice that bore no trace of friendliness.

"Hope he got his facts right," Jeko said with an edgy laugh.

The laugh died away as Tuller turned his steady stare on to Jeko. "I wouldn't know," Tuller said. "Facts're things can be *proved*. All I been hearin' is stories. 'Bout people on other planets, an' spaceships, an' rebels . . ." He shrugged huge sloping shoulders. "I never liked science fiction much."

"What do you . . ." Heleth began hotly, but fell silent at a sharp gesture from Samella.

"It's not fiction," Cord said firmly. "If Stele told you what we told him, it's truth."

"So you say," Tuller replied. "But I don't take folks' word on things. *Facts*, that's what I go on." His gaze swung round the room before fastening on Cord. "Fact is I got a couple Streeters back, Jeko an' Rontal, but I don't know—for a *fact*—where they been. Fact is they come back with three strangers, an' I don't know for a *fact* who or what they are. But they come askin' us to go to some planet an' fight somebody else's war for 'em. And I gotta take their *word* for it all."

Rontal, like Cord, had not moved—but his tall body seemed to gather itself, like a spring being wound. "The word of two Streeters," he growled. "We don't lie to our own."

Tuller studied him coldly. "Maybe. You an' Jeko were Streeters 'fore you got lifted, sure. You still look like Streeters. But what're you now, *inside*?"

"What we always were," Jeko flared. "I figure Stele found that out last night. Found out what our friends are, too."

Tuller merely stared. "Maybe," he repeated. "Stele says you did pretty good in the fight. But that proves nothin'. You *had* to join in, to get on the good side of me an' the troop."

"Doesn't seem to have worked," Rontal snarled.

"If you need proof about us," Samella said coolly, "what about Cord and Heleth? You must know that even ordinary people don't travel much, without a lot of special permission and checking. If our story isn't true, how could a Highlander and a Bunker Vampire get into an American city?"

"Easy," Tuller rasped, "if you're part of a CeeDee trick—to draw the Streeters outa Limbo an' finish us off."

10

Prisoners of Limbo

"That's *sick!*" Heleth exploded, and took a lunging step towards Tuller. But she found her way barred by Cord's powerful arm—and then Jeko intervened, looking no less furious.

"You're sayin' we're *planted* by the CeeDees?" he demanded. "You've known me and Rontal all our lives!"

Tuller shrugged. "You were lifted by the Cee-Dees—I know *that*. An' CeeDees got ways to twist folks' minds. There've been Streeters who've been lifted an' ended up wearin' CeeDee uniform."

Jeko seemed to grow speechless with rage just as Cord found his voice, despite his own anger. "The five of us have more reason to hate the CeeDees—and ColSec—than anyone else in Limbo," he said. "That you can believe."

"On what proof?" Tuller sneered.

"On the fact that we're *here*," Samella said hotly. "Would the CeeDees be likely to invent a story like that? They would have made up a story that you *would* believe—and they would have sent Jeko and Rontal on their own, to set it up."

Tuller frowned, dismissing her logic. "We've done enough talkin'," he snarled. "I say that you bein' CeeDee plants is a *lot* more likely than you bein' some kinda outer space rebels. But it don't matter anyway. 'Cause the Streeters are stayin' in Limbo. This is our place, where we run things, an' what happens somewhere else—on Earth or wherever—got nothin' to do with us."

"So that's it," Cord said harshly. "You don't care who we are one way or another. You just want to stay nice and safe in your Limbo rat's-nest."

Samella nodded, her eyes bright with anger. "It's a power thing, isn't it, Tuller? You don't *want* to believe us, because some of your Streeters might want to join us. Maybe most of them. And then you wouldn't be chief anymore. You're afraid you'd lose your power, your little kingdom, if the Streeters leave Limbo."

Tuller's eyes had darkened with rage. "I said we've done enough talkin'. Streeters aren't leavin' Limbo—not one of 'em. Even if some are stupid enough to believe what you say." He swung his baleful stare towards Stele. "The three strangers stay here, under guard. Rontal an' Jeko can come out an' hang around with the others if they want—but they get watched, every minute. Your job, Stele. You watch 'em good."

Then he wheeled and strode out of the cellar.

For a moment Stele hung back, looking upset. "I told your story as fairly as I could," he said. "And about last night. But I could see what was happening as I was telling him. Just like Samella said. Here he's the chief—so here we stay."

"I suppose if we had all the proof in the world," Samella said, "he'd refuse to believe us. Because we're a threat to his power."

"Probably," Stele agreed. "He knows that lots of us are interested in the idea of another world, and the freedom..." His voice sounded wistful. "Till you folk came along, I thought like Tuller. That Streeters belong in Limbo, because here we run our own lives, free. But now..."

"No one's really free on Earth while the Organization runs it," Samella said quietly. "Not even in Limbo. CeeDees are always prowling around the edges. It's like a big prison, and you've all got life sentences."

"Right," Heleth put in. "I felt that going back to the Bunkers. Never thought about it before—but if anyone sticks their nose outside, like I did once, CeeDees are all over them."

Stele nodded gloomily. "That's how a lot of us feel now. You come talking about a free, open planet where we can live how we want...Limbo starts looking like a miserable dead end, compared to that. A place like your world—it'd be worth fighting for."

"Fighting Tuller?" Cord asked pointedly.

Stele shrugged. "He's still chief. The Streeters will do what he tells them."

"Chiefs can be challenged in any troop," Heleth said angrily. "I'll take the big yeck-head on."

"You wouldn't have a chance," Stele said. "None of us would. He's too big and too mean, and he could give Crushers lessons in combat. He's been challenged once or twice, and he didn't just win. The challengers got buried, in pieces."

"Do we get buried too?" Samella asked flatly.

"Maybe Tuller will cool off," Stele replied, "and let you go after a while. I'll see what I can do when he calms down." He looked around at them all. "It would have been something, going on a spaceship, having a share of a new world."

He turned away, and reluctantly Jeko and Rontal went with him. Cord heard a key turn in the stout cellar door, as other Streeters took up positions as guards, just outside.

"Let's hope the Streeters won't be needed in the army on Klydor," Samella said bitterly.

Heleth scowled. "It's so stupid. We come to ask them to help us fight ColSec, and we end up fighting them."

"Not fighting," Cord said heavily. "Just trying

to get away, however we can. Because Lathan will bring the spaceship back looking for us—*tonight.*"

Time dragged forward slowly during that day, and almost nothing interrupted the monotony of the cellar. Once, at midday, their guards brought food, but otherwise the three prisoners sat in empty silence, wrapped in misery. By the day's end, as dusk fell once again upon the city, Cord's nerves and temper were fraying badly. But it was Heleth who erupted to her feet.

"Much more of this and I'll go through the walls!" she snarled.

Cord smiled mirthlessly at the concrete walls and the solid door. "I wish you could. But maybe we should try to jump the guards when they bring food next. With Heleth's eyes we might get away in the dark."

Samella looked doubtful, but Heleth brightened. Then they all froze, at a sudden tap on the cellar door.

"Cord!" It was Stele's voice, in a penetrating whisper.

"Still here," Cord said sourly.

"Something's happening," Stele said, sounding anxious. "Tuller went away earlier, didn't say where, but when he got back he looked pleased with himself—like he does when he's hurt somebody. And now he's told us we're moving, to another part of Limbo."

"Leaving us here?" Cord asked tensely.

"Looks that way," Stele said. "Nobody knows what's going on, and Rontal and Jeko got into trouble trying to find out. But Tuller's even pulled your guards away. I don't like it—and I wish I could help you."

"Can't you get us out?" Cord demanded.

"No—Tuller's got the key," Stele said. "And I have to join the others before he gets suspicious." He paused. "I'm really sorry. And I wish I could have seen that planet."

The three stared at each other fearfully as Stele's light footsteps faded away, outside.

"What could Tuller be up to?" Heleth wondered.

"That's the question," Samella said. "What would make him come back acting pleased with himself?" A small frown creased her brow. "And why is he moving the Streeters?"

"Because something is going to happen here," Cord said, almost without thinking. "To us."

Then his eyes widened at the thought of what those words could mean, and Samella drew her breath in sharply.

"That's it!" she said in a rush. "The CeeDees! Tuller must have got to them, and sold us out!"

Heleth said something vicious under her breath.

"Maybe he did a deal," Samella went on. "The CeeDees get us and agree to leave the Streeters alone for a while. Or maybe he got paid."

Cord glowered as he thought about it. It was the most logical explanation for Tuller's strange behaviour.

It was also wholly sickening. "A good thing Jeko didn't tell Stele all the details about where Lathan will land," he growled.

"That doesn't help *us*," Heleth said sharply. "How do we get out of here?"

His temper ablaze, Cord strode to the door and delivered a thunderous kick. But the door's solid frame was set firmly in the concrete wall, and it only rattled slightly.

"Could we chip the concrete away around it?" Samella ventured.

"Not without tools," Cord said shortly. "And it's nearly too dark for anyone but Heleth to see."

They glanced up, seeing that the light filtering between the planks of the ceiling was nearly gone. Then they paused and looked again.

"The ceiling," Samella said.

"Maybe," Cord said, brightening. "Some of the boards could be rotten. But how do we get up there?"

Heleth squared her sturdy shoulders. "You stand on us, muscle man."

Cord blinked, then nodded. Pulling off his boots, using the wall to keep his balance, he planted a foot carefully on the shoulder of each girl as they crouched down. Then they slowly straightened, trembling with the effort, lifting him up. Cord glanced down to be sure that they were solidly braced.

"Here goes," he said.

Taking a deep breath, he struck furiously up at one board of the ceiling, using the heel of his hand. The board quivered, but did not give a millimetre.

Angrily, Cord slammed his hand upwards again, ignoring the pain of bruised flesh. Again the board did not budge.

"Not going to work, is it?" Heleth said heavily.

The disappointment in her voice, and Samella's sympathetic upward glance, seemed to stab into Cord like a hot wire. His fiery temper flared again—directed at everything that stood in his way. Tuller, the CeeDees, the monstrous city, the imprisoning cellar—all of them mingled into a common enemy, there before him to be struck down.

The girls told him later that the muscles of his back seemed to swell to twice their size, and that he had given a chilling yell, as his hand smashed upwards for the third time. The impact was so ferocious that the reaction drove both girls to their knees, and all of them went sprawling on the cellar floor.

But where Cord's hand had struck that raging, thunderous blow, the board of the ceiling had lifted and splintered, with a screech of twisted nails.

A gap had been created. Swiftly, ignoring their painful shoulders, the girls hoisted Cord up again. And now he could grip the adjoining board, two-handed, and heave mightily to wrench it loose. Moments later, there was a space large enough for them to crawl through.

Cord dropped to the floor, pulled on his boots, then lifted the girls in turn so they could grasp the edge of the hole and wriggle their way upwards.

Then he leaped high, catching the edge with his fingers, pulling himself up.

They were out, free and unseen, with the darkness of Limbo gathering around them.

11

Flight to Disaster

"Wish we could run into that Tuller," Heleth muttered. "Don't care how tough he is—I'd tear his throat out."

"A few Streeters might feel the same," Cord said, "if he did turn us in and the CeeDees come to get us."

"Let's not wait to find out," Samella urged.

They moved away swiftly, Heleth in the lead, picking a winding path through the dark and ruined streets. But almost at once their relief at being free was replaced by a growing worry about whether they were on the *right* streets. All of them had relied on Jeko and Rontal to lead them in the right direction, across the city. And Cord especially was furious with himself for not having paid more attention to possible landmarks along the route. His wilderness tracking skills and sense of direction were nearly useless in the city. Every crumbling side street looked much like every other, or at least equally unfamiliar.

Finally, after about two hours of hurrying through the night, they paused to take stock.

"We could be heading in completely the wrong direction," Cord said gloomily.

"Let's get to the edge of the city and circle round it," Heleth suggested.

"We don't have time," Samella said. "Not if we come out of the city on the far side from where Lathan will land."

Cord stared around, desperately hoping for the sight of something familiar in the shadowy surroundings. Then he tensed. Heleth had clutched his arm and Samella's, dragging them into deeper darkness behind a heap of rubble.

At first Cord saw nothing. But then he glimpsed the movement that had alerted the cat-eyed Heleth. Three moving blobs of lighter shadow, within the darkness of the street—blobs that Cord could identify.

The spiky white hair of three Hatchetmen.

Cord sighed to himself with relief. If they had come into Hatchetman territory, they were on the right route. The fact that it was a dangerous place to be hardly reduced his pleasure.

The three blobs moved on, disappearing around a corner. Then Heleth led them carefully forward, listening hard. "Can't be too many of them around," she whispered, "after that fight. We got lucky."

We'd better stay that way, Cord said silently to

himself. He glanced up at the sky, noting the positions of a few stars visible through ragged cloud. That would keep them on course, moving in the same direction they had taken since leaving the cellar, which should bring them out of the city somewhere near Lathan's landing place.

Heleth froze again, and Cord's heart leaped with alarm. All three of them could hear the new sound—the distant rumble of CeeDee vehicles.

"Lots of them—but not coming this way." Heleth's voice sounded harsh with anger. "They're heading for where we were—in Limbo."

"So Tuller did turn us in," Cord said bleakly.

"Let's move, fast," Samella said. "When they find we're gone, they'll start a major search. We have to keep ahead of it if we can."

They fled, as swiftly as darkness and strange terrain would allow. The night seemed to blur into a succession of squalid streets and reeking alleys, as they dashed along, holding as best they could to the course Cord had plotted. And as they flitted through the streets, the sounds behind them showed that Samella had been right.

The CeeDees had begun to scour the city for the fugitives.

For some time the search seemed to be concentrated on Limbo, far behind them, so they were able to extend their head start. But eventually, after an hour or more, the searchers began to spread their net wider.

During the next hours, there seemed to be a

floater around every corner, a hovertank at the end of every street. Many times Heleth dragged them into cover just before a CeeDee flyer soared overhead, spotlights probing down like prying fingers. Every moment that they remained undetected seemed miraculous.

Yet the miracles continued to happen. The floaters turned the wrong corners, skimming off in the wrong directions. The hovertanks roared too swiftly past the dark corners where they huddled, or crashed thunderously into derelict houses that sheltered only a few terrified mice.

And, judging by the noise of vehicles that they could hear but not see, a large part of the search still seemed to be concentrated behind them.

"We've come farther than they expect," Samella guessed. "They're looking for us where we've been."

"Maybe," Heleth said, and surprised them all by stifling a giggle. "But there's lots of tanks and floaters roaring around one spot back there. I figure they've spotted some Hatchetmen, and they're chasing *them*!"

The humour, amid the tension, struck Cord and Samella just as strongly. And had anyone been there to see, they would have been amazed at the sight of three young fugitives running for their lives, yet choking with laughter as they ran.

But the laughter soon died, when the next CeeDee flyer whisked overhead. They continued their frantic, furtive race, street after street, building after building. The moment of laughter was soon forgotten, in the relentless succession of desperate near-misses and frantic escapes.

The CeeDees were hampered, Cord came to realize, by the fact that they doggedly remained in their vehicles—because that was the way they always patrolled the city. And the vehicles moved too swiftly, unable to pry into every cranny, every patch of blackness. It seemed as if the CeeDees had not been told, or were ignoring, the fact that one of the runaways was a Bunker girl with uncanny night sight and hearing. Nor, of course, did the CeeDees have any idea what route the fugitives would be following—so their manpower had to be spread out in every direction from Limbo.

So the three ran or crept onwards, eluding all the vehicles that stormed past them, guided by the stars and protected by Heleth's nocturnal abilities.

And before too long, they found themselves in the midst of one of the areas where the poorer denizens of the city lived—the shabby four-storey boxes, row upon dismal row. There, where the lighting was almost as non-existent as in Limbo, they could increase their pace a little—ignoring the weariness of their legs, the growing fire in their lungs. The fringes of the city were not far away, and that knowledge gave them new strength. So did the fact that the search had again fallen behind them, so that for half an hour they scarcely saw a vehicle except for some distant flyers.

Oddly, the lessening of the search seemed to

worry Samella. "It's as if they've stopped trying too hard," she said.

"Fine with me," Heleth muttered.

"They're probably not used to trying hard," Cord suggested. "Like Lathan said—they feel invulnerable. They just can't believe we can get away."

"Maybe," Samella said, sounding unconvinced. "But it scares me. I can't put my finger on it—but what if the CeeDees *know* something, so that they don't have to try too hard?"

Puzzled and uneasy, Cord would have pursued the subject—but he was distracted. The street they were on had begun to narrow into a grubby lane, and they discovered that it was leading to the city's outskirts. Around them only a few other miserable lanes straggled out among weed-filled fields, junk yards, stinking rubbish dumps and all the debris that gathers on a city's fringe like flotsam on a beach.

They paused briefly, trying to match their surroundings with what they recalled of the edge of the city on their inward trip. In the end they agreed, hesitantly, that the place they were seeking probably lay some way to the south. They crept guardedly on, even more aware—after Samella's ominous words— that no CeeDee searchers seemed to be anywhere in the vicinity. But then again elation diverted their thoughts.

Heleth's night vision still guided their steps, but it was Cord's lifetime in wild country that allowed him—even in the minimal glimmer of starlight—to

identify a familiar formation of scrub pines and
tangled brush.

They had made it. Within that brush lay the
empty patch of wasteland where Lathan had first
landed the ship, to launch them into the city.

Cord glanced up at the stars and smiled with
satisfaction. "We couldn't have done better if Rontal
and Jeko were with us."

"Wish they were," Heleth said sadly.

That caused a long gloomy silence, as they
pushed through the tangled scrub and stepped out on
to the wasteland. Again Cord looked up and became
nervously aware of the first faint grey streaks appearing
over the city, in the eastern sky. The third dawn
since we landed, Cord thought. And a sudden wave
of utter desolation washed over him, as he thought of
how they would soon be lifting off again—without
any Streeters to help in the fight for Klydor, but
especially without the two Streeters who had become
two of the closest friends he would ever have.

Heleth nudged him, and he realized that he
could hear an incredibly distant whisper of sound. It
grew rapidly, and Cord tensed, wondering if it was
the engine of an approaching hovertank. But then
he relaxed, and the three of them stared upwards at
the speck of flame falling through the sky towards
them.

It swelled with astonishing speed, as did the
howl of the spaceship's engines. In only moments,
the great ship was settling in a storm of flame and
dust, the engines were dying to a muted rumble, and

from the airlock Bren Lathan was springing lightly to the ground.

His face was tight with disappointment and concern, for obviously he would have seen through the scanners that no horde of Streeters awaited him on that wasteland—only three of his five young friends.

"We were betrayed," Samella explained, and began to tell Lathan about Tuller and their escape.

But in the growing light of the dawn Cord saw Lathan turn white, his eyes wild.

"Get into the ship!" he shouted. "This place will be full of CeeDees, any second!"

Cord and the girls hesitated, wide-eyed. "They don't know where you're landing," Cord said. "Jeko didn't say . . ."

"They'll know that a ship is landing somewhere!" Lathan snapped, herding them to the ship. "They'll have been monitoring all spaceflights near the city, since the Streeter chief betrayed you—and they'll have spotted me as soon as I entered atmosphere!"

"But how would they know to come here?" Cord asked, still hesitating.

And then Samella startled them, slapping her hand to her head in despair. "I *knew* there was something," she wailed. "I couldn't think straight back there. If they spotted your ship, ColSec would lock a computer on to it!"

"Right," Lathan said, pushing them forward. "The computer could plot my course and work out my landing place before I got here. They *know* where we are!"

As if in dire echo of his words, they all could suddenly hear the distant, menacing rumble of CeeDee machines, approaching at top speed.

They flung themselves through the airlock and Lathan leaped for the controls. Cord heard a burst of thunder that seemed to be the great ship responding. But then he saw that Lathan had not yet touched his instruments. Instead, his hands dropped, and he stared upwards, his face as cold and bleak as a death mask.

The thunder was coming from outside. And immediately Cord saw its source, surging into sight through the viewport. The rounded bulk of a space shuttle, hovering above them on its retros—and bristling with the evil muzzles of laser cannon.

"They tracked me and sent a gun-ship," Lathan said hollowly.

They all jumped as the ship's communicator snapped into life. Cord felt that metal bands were tightening around him, preventing him from moving or breathing, as he listened to the coldly satisfied voice coming from the speaker.

"This is Commander Itzil of the Civil Defenders," the voice said. "If you try to start your engines, we will fire. Remain where you are. You are my prisoners."

12

Prisoners of ColSec

The two girls slumped down, ashen faces twisted with horror at the sudden crushing collapse of their hopes. But Cord still sat like a statue, every muscle clenched, while within him grew not horror or despair but a wild, volcanic rage.

"Do not try to leave the ship," continued the cold voice on the communicator. "My forces are surrounding the area. If you try to escape, or resist, you will be shot."

Lathan half-turned, glancing towards a laserifle clipped to the metal wall of the ship. As he began to rise, Cord also stood up, his berserk fury flaming in his eyes.

"Cord, Bren, *don't*!" Samella's voice was almost a shriek. "You won't help by getting killed!"

"We're already dead," Lathan said flatly. "So...we take as many with us as we can."

"No!" Samella insisted, leaping up in front of them. "We're *not* dead yet—and we're not finished while we're still alive!"

"Nobody escapes from a CeeDee prison," Heleth growled, looking around for a weapon.

"We've done a lot of things lately that no one's done before!" Samella snapped. "We can't just commit suicide in a blaze of glory! That's giving up!"

"Samella..." Lathan began, reaching out to move her aside.

But he did not complete the motion. The airlock hissed open, and the interior of the ship was suddenly filled with a riot of blue uniforms.

Cord and the others stood frozen for an instant under the overwhelming shock of that assault. Then Cord saw Samella twist aside from a grasping CeeDee hand, saw the hand close into a fist and slam against the side of her head, turning her eyes glassy. And the red tidal wave of fury within Cord mounted higher, and erupted.

Two CeeDees had gripped him, but he broke from their grasp as if their hands were dry twigs. His fist swung like a pile-driver, burying itself to the wrist in the belly of the man who had struck Samella. The man crumpled, retching, as other blue uniforms flung themselves on Cord. But he hurled them aside like feathers, lashing out wildly with his fists. The maddened blows fell like hammers, and men tumbled away on every side with shattered faces and crushed ribs. But always there were more, and more, crowding in through the airlock.

And at last, inevitably, though Cord fought on with the speed and strength of a maddened demon, there was one too many. He did not see the clubbing gun butt that caused the burst of pain and light within his head. He did not even feel his legs giving way and was still trying to strike one last blow as the murky darkness gathered him in.

He awoke with some surprise. When he thought about the manic battle—as much as he could think through the searing ache in his skull—he knew that he had not expected to emerge alive. But alive he was, and there was some small comfort in that. As there was in the knowledge that he had offered some resistance, rather than surrendering meekly.

But then he remembered Heleth's grim words— that no one escaped from a CeeDee prison. And there was no comfort to be found when he opened his eyes. He was lying—clothed only in his underwear— on a narrow hard bed in a narrow grey room. Above him a small high window displayed solid metal bars, and the dark metal door hummed faintly as if it was electrified.

He was not shackled in any way, but it took all his determination to raise himself from that bed. His whole body felt battered, and the ache in his head made his eyes lose focus as he swung his feet to the floor. But he gritted his teeth, fought the wave of pain and weakness and stood.

The effort had little point. The walls were solid,

the window too high to reach, and touching the door would surely kill him. Then he saw the grey bundle by the door, near a low panel that probably opened. It turned out to be a dull grey coverall, his own boots, and a small container of tepid water. He felt slightly better when he was dressed, and the water served to push the headache back to a bearable level.

But as he returned to sit on the bed, a far greater pain swept through him—an anguish that came with the final realization that there was no hope, that all the dreams of freedom he and his friends had dreamed on Klydor had been destroyed.

He knew that, elsewhere in the grim building, Lathan and the two girls would be in similar lonely cells, each of them also facing the soul-crushing fact of their defeat. He knew he would probably never see them again, or Rontal and Jeko, or Klydor—or even whatever part of Earth lay beyond the walls that held him. He had no doubt that he was facing a sentence of death. Even if he was punished merely with imprisonment, being caged would affect him as it would any creature of the open spaces. He would quickly fall into mindlessness or madness. In his consuming despair, he found himself almost hoping for a quick end to his life.

Then, through that despair, he heard as if from a distance the scrape of metal upon metal. He looked up dully and saw that another, higher panel in the door had opened, to reveal a heavy metal grille. And through the grille he saw a face, watching him.

A CeeDee guard's face, of course—jowly and lumpy, with small wet eyes and a lipless mouth as wide as a toad's.

" 'Bout time you woke up," the guard said.

Ignoring him, Cord turned his head to stare at the opposite wall.

"You don't look like much," the guard went on, his toad-mouth opening in a loose grin. "Just a kid. What kinda rebellion can ya have with a buncha weird scards?"

A flash of anger rose in Cord at the word—the CeeDee name for the young outlaws sent into space by ColSec: "discards". But he clenched his teeth and kept silent.

"Not talkin', eh?" the toad went on, still grinning. "Don' matter. You'll do all the talkin' that's needed, 'fore the trial."

That word lifted Cord's head sharply. "Trial?" he croaked.

The toad laughed uproariously. "Thought that'd getcha," he said. "Sure, a trial. Goin' to be on the vid, world-wide. Ever'body's goin' to be shown what happens to scards who go to be rebels." Another burst of laughter. "You gonna be *famous*, kid. The vid-cameras are gonna stay with alla you, through the trial an' after. Right up to the execution!"

For a long time after the guard had gone, Cord sat staring unseeingly at the wall of his cell. The blank numbness within him had not been caused by the confirmation that he was to be executed. He had expected nothing else, for himself or the others. His mind had merely retreated into itself, had in a way shut down, so as to stop going over the bitter knowledge that the dream of freedom on Klydor had ended in the cruel reality of a CeeDee cell.

But during that day of motionless misery, the toad-like guard did everything he could to make things worse.

Shortly, he returned with a bowl of food, which he thrust sloppily through the lower panel in the door. Cord glanced once at the grey, soupy contents, felt nauseated and ignored it. And the toad found that highly amusing too.

"Not hungry?" he asked. "Guess ya don't needta keep yer strength up. Not where yer goin'."

More bellows of laughter, with the toad-mouth seeming to stretch back to the ears. Cord stared straight ahead, oblivious.

"Here's some'p'n else ta think about," the toad went on. "A big detachment of Crushers is gettin' ready ta go inta Limbo. Them Streeters been runnin' around too long, thinkin' they can get away with everythin'. Crushers're gonna wipe 'em out, fer good."

Cord's eyes flickered at that news. If Tuller had made some deal with the CeeDees when he betrayed Cord and the girls, the CeeDees were clearly not keeping their side of it. It seemed a sort of rough justice—the betrayer betrayed. But that, too, held no comfort for Cord. The Crushers—that murderous elite of immensely skilled killers—would not stop until they had remorselessly hunted down every Streeter in Limbo. And that would include Rontal and Jeko.

As that terrible day wore on, Cord's black fatalism took over completely. At times he felt that he already knew what death was like. He felt himself to be a ghost, an empty husk, doomed to sit forever in a bare and gloomy cell, while the toad-guard went on stirring up in his mind those images that he could not bear to see.

"Heard some more news," the toad said, grinning through the grille again in the early afternoon. "ColSec's gettin' a fleet ready. Goin' inta space to take all them rebels by surprise. And after, from now on, gonna be CeeDees on every planet. No more rebellions, kid. Ever. Whatcha think 'bout that?"

Cord did not reply. The colony worlds hardly seemed real to him now—more like things that had existed long ago, in another life. But some small part of his mind wondered whether the rebels could have somehow learned about the betrayal and the capture of Lathan's ship. If so, they might already have begun the destruction and evacuation of the colonies, taking their populations to Klydor to join the small—too small, perhaps—army that had been recruited.

At least, Cord knew, Tuller the traitor could not have told the CeeDees much about the rebel plans, for neither he nor Stele had known many details. So

ColSec would still not be aware of what might be waiting for them—defences prepared on Klydor and a small squadron of rebel spaceships—when its fleet went into space.

But even that knowledge offered scant comfort. Neither Cord nor his friends were likely to be still alive when ColSec came up against the true extent of the rebellion.

Many hours later, as night closed in around the prison and a single stark light flicked on from the high ceiling of his cell, Cord shifted position and lay down—only to stare just as unseeingly at the ceiling. Eventually he drifted into a half-sleep, with scarcely any difference between one kind of mental shutdown and another. But his eyes were open again, fixed on the ceiling, when morning brought the toad-guard back to grin stupidly through the grille.

But this time there was another face at the grille. A lean face, with angry eyes, a scarred and cruel mouth—and beneath it the blue uniform and bright insignia of a CeeDee officer. And the officer's voice was the one that Cord had heard on the communicator, when Lathan's ship had been stopped from taking off.

"Hasn't said nothin', Commander Itzil," the toad said, his voice heavily respectful.

"A common reaction," Itzil said coldly. "He will be saying a great deal, very soon."

He gestured to the toad, who pressed the heavy door's controls. As it slid open, the two of them entered the cell—with three more CeeDees crowding behind them, electrical stunner-guns in their hands.

"On yer feet," the toad snarled.

Slowly Cord rose, his eyes fixed on Itzil. Something in that gaze made the commander take an involuntary step backwards. But then he caught himself and barked an angry order. One of the other CeeDees moved forward, to fasten a body-restrainer on to Cord, clamping his arms to his sides.

"Let's go," the toad growled.

"Where?" Cord said, breaking his silence at last. "To the *trial*?"

Itzil smiled viciously, ignoring the irony in Cord's voice. "Not yet. You're being transferred to ColSec Central Headquarters. You and your friends are to be interrogated—with every advanced means available—until we have extracted all the details of this so-called rebellion."

Cord might have expected something of the sort, but the words fell on him with a new avalanche of despair. He knew something of CeeDee methods of interrogation, enough to know that he and the others would not be able to resist. Soon, then, ColSec would know all the plans of the rebellion. And the rebels would be doomed.

Within the restrainer his muscles tensed, hopelessly seeking to break free. But the three other CeeDees levelled their stunner-guns and thrust him towards the door.

"Walk out quiet," one of them snapped, "or we burn yer kneecaps off an' carry ya."

Cord glared at them. But, because he wanted to stand and face his enemies for as long as he could during the terrors to come, he merely turned away, lifted his head and strode expressionlessly out of the cell.

13

Death on the Streets

Cord was herded through the corridors of the prison by the three CeeDees, leaving the toad and Commander Itzil behind. Outside the prison, on a sweep of empty concrete, stood an immense vehicle—heavily armoured and with the same aproned base as a hovertank, but ten times larger. The huge rear doors, standing open, showed that it was some kind of special transporter. Armed CeeDees sat in the driver's compartment and in the protected gun turret on top of the vehicle, and more hard-faced CeeDees with guns stood watchfully around the area.

A savage push from one of his guards sent Cord stumbling into the transporter. And there, on a bench running along one side, sat Samella, Heleth and Lathan, all wearing body restrainers.

Their greetings were muted by the presence of

the CeeDees outside, and by their knowledge of where the giant vehicle would be taking them. As Cord settled on to the bench, Lathan peered out through the doors.

"Seems to be a delay," he said dryly.

"We're in no hurry," Heleth growled.

Cord grasped at the chance to compare information. "A guard told me that a ColSec fleet is going to attack the colonies," he said.

The others nodded. "We heard that," Lathan said. "But it'll take them a while to get it ready. And the rebels will know by now that we were captured. So no matter what we're forced to tell ColSec, the rebels won't be taken by surprise. They'll be evacuating the colonies now. And it might be ColSec that runs into a surprise attack, from our ships in space."

But before they could say anything more, they were interrupted by a mighty thunder. Through the doors they saw another of the giant hover-transporters sweeping across the concrete.

"This may be what we're waiting for," Lathan said. "More prisoners, going the same way."

"They could be Streeters," Samella guessed, "captured in the raid on Limbo. Did you hear about that, Cord?"

Cord nodded, as they watched the second transporter draw up behind their own vehicle. "Hope some of them got away," he muttered.

"Two in particular," Heleth growled.

But then Cord's three CeeDee guards stepped

into their transporter, and the heavy doors swung shut as the giant engine started up.

"Awright, shut it," one of the guards snapped. "Any talkin' an' you'll be chewin' on yer teeth."

The CeeDees settled themselves on the bench opposite the prisoners as the transporter surged smoothly forward. Close behind, they could hear the muffled thunder of the second machine. As they swept steadily along, Cord began to try to visualize what part of the city they might be passing through. But he soon abandoned that, for it called up too many memories of their own frightening treks through those mazy streets. Instead, he began working out how many people the vast transporter could contain, if filled. In the end he guessed that about a hundred and twenty might be crammed in. The four of them and the three guards seemed almost lost in that space.

That led him to consider vague and hopeless ideas of how the four of them, without the use of their arms, might overpower the guards and somehow escape from the vehicle. He hatched half a dozen wild plans, each of them absurdly impossible. But it passed the time and kept him from thinking too much about what awaited them at ColSec Central.

At that point, his thoughts were startlingly interrupted.

From above, where the transporter's gun-turret was placed, he heard the sudden searing hiss of laser fire—several quick bursts. The guards sat up, wide-eyed, reaching for their stunner-guns.

Then the air outside was torn apart by a titanic explosion that seemed loud enough to be the end of the world.

The giant transporter heaved and swerved, the shriek of tortured metal mingling with the echoes of the blast. Then the entire immense mass of the machine seemed to leap slightly into the air—before toppling over with a crumpling crash on to its side.

Cord and his friends were flung bruisingly backwards, against the wall of the transporter that was now beneath them. But the restrainers that gripped them also served as padding to protect them as they slammed against the metal. At the same time the three guards were hurled forward, falling from their side of the vehicle, which was now above the prisoners.

Their helmets and uniform armour protected them, as well, but not enough. They did not recover as quickly as the prisoners—and so they did not recover at all. Cord and his friends used their boots with savage ferocity, until all three CeeDees lay crumpled and unconscious.

But that did not improve the prisoners' position. Their arms were still firmly clamped, and they had no way of reaching the key to the restrainers, or the guards' guns, that were there for the taking. Outside, they could still hear the raking sizzle of laser weapons. They could not guess what was happening—but the wreck of the transporter had rekindled hope within them all. They struggled frantically against the unyielding restrainers, but stopped, hearts sinking, as the great doors of the vehicle were wrenched open.

All four turned like hunted animals at bay. But they stiffened with shock when they saw who was manhandling the doors.

Three hairless youths with blood on their clothes, guns in their hands and startled expressions on their faces. Rontal and Jeko—and Stele.

"What in all the stars . . ." Lathan breathed.

"We mined the street," Stele said quickly as they leaped inside. "The other transporter's carrying about a hundred Streeters, prisoners. We figured this one was, too."

"Thought you folk were dead, for sure," Jeko said as he found the key to the restrainers and freed them.

"We thought *you* were!" Heleth said. "They told us Crushers went in to clear out Limbo!"

"They did," Rontal growled. "But Stele got about fifty of us out, safe—with most of the Streeters' store of weapons."

"Tell us later," Lathan said urgently. "What's happening outside?"

"We sort of finished off the CeeDees," Jeko said with a fierce grin. "And our boys'll be handin' out guns to the Streeters we set free . . ."

"Then let's move!" Lathan said. He scooped up the gun of one of the fallen guards, and Cord and

Heleth took the others. "There'll be flyers here any second, and an army of CeeDees not far behind!"

Stele grinned calmly. "You're Lathan, the pilot, right?" As Lathan nodded, he went on. "You can relax—the Streeters know what to do. They'll pick off any flyers that show, and we'll disappear into the city before floaters or tanks get here."

Lathan subsided, looking rueful. "Sorry—Stele. You're in charge."

But Cord looked dubious, thinking of the frightening pursuit that would follow, as every available CeeDee—and Crusher—scoured the city for them. "Isn't there some·other way?" he asked.

"Yes!" Samella suddenly cried. "Stele, get *all* the Streeters *inside* the other transporter, and tell them not to fire at anything! Cord, Bren, get into a couple of these uniforms!" She gestured at the fallen guards. "Stele, you and some Streeters get into other CeeDee uniforms, and get into the driver's seat and the turret of the other transporter! When CeeDees get here, this situation is going to seem under *control*!"

They all stared, realization dawning, and Cord laughed with delight to see Samella's cool intelligence working in overdrive.

"It could work!" Lathan said excitedly, as a grinning Stele leaped from the transporter to give the orders.

"But if we take the transporter," Heleth demanded, "where do we go?"

Lathan's laugh was reckless. "Where else? To the ColSec spaceport—and steal a *ship*!"

· · ·

Cord and Lathan changed their clothes in frantic seconds and leaped out of the overturned transporter. The other giant vehicle, looking unharmed, stood silent with its doors closed. But blue-uniformed Streeters, helmets hiding their shaven heads, were taking their places at the controls and the gun turret.

And just in time. A flyer screamed down over the rooftops, slamming on to the concrete near the transporters. Four CeeDees, helmet visors up to reveal the tattoo insignia of the dreaded Crushers, leaped from the machine, deadly sun-guns in their hands. Their cold eyes took in the wrecked transporter, the scattering of Streeter and CeeDee bodies, and then the uniformed figures of Cord and Lathan.

"Streeter attack, sir," Lathan said, sounding respectful. "But we drove them off. All prisoners still secure—we put them together in the one transporter."

The leader of the Crusher team studied him for a heart-stopping moment, then nodded. "Good work," he said casually. He leaned into the flyer, apparently reporting on the machine's communicator, while Cord and Lathan held their breath.

Then he emerged, his eyes still cold. "We'll escort you the rest of the way, in the flyer," he said. "Those street rats might try it again."

"I don't think . . ." Lathan began anxiously.

"Those are *orders*, fella," the Crusher barked. "What's wrong with you?"

Lathan glanced despairingly at Cord. If the flyer went with them, their plan was wrecked. But the only way to prevent it was to fight the Crushers—and they had no chance against the sun-guns and the trained skills of the four killers. Yet Cord saw that Lathan was going to go for his gun, and he braced himself to do the same, knowing he would be dead before he could fire.

But he did not move. Without warning, the lasers in the transporter's turret blazed. The Crushers began to whirl, sun-guns blasting—but their shots went wild as the laser cut them down before they could take proper aim.

Shakily, Cord turned from the four bodies and saw Stele pushing the turret open, grinning.

"Cold-blooded, but effective," Lathan remarked dryly, as he and Cord snatched up the four sun-guns from the fallen Crushers.

"I'm not complaining," Cord said.

"If we take the corpses in the transporter, we can use the flyer," Lathan said. "The CeeDees won't suspect anything—for a while."

Cord grinned and beckoned to Stele. Only seconds later the dead Crushers had been stowed in the transporter with the Streeters, and Lathan and Cord were leaping for the flyer, with the two girls and Jeko and Rontal.

"You're not gettin' away from us again," Jeko announced as they scrambled into the flyer.

"It's a four-man flyer..." Lathan began.

"Samella and me together weigh less'n one big CeeDee," Jeko told him. "And ol' Heleth doesn't look as fat as she used to."

"If we live through this," Heleth said with a scowl, "you'll wish you hadn't said that."

Then they were flung back in their seats as Lathan swept the flyer upwards, while below them the transporter roared forward, away from the corpse-littered battle scene.

For a while they had a breathing space, thanks to the report on the communicator from the Crusher, stating that everything was secure. There were other flyers in the area, and plenty of floaters and hovertanks rushing through the streets below. But the CeeDees were searching the area around the scene of the attack, where they believed armed Streeters would still be lurking.

So there was time for Rontal and Jeko to tell the others what had happened in Limbo, after Cord and the girls had been imprisoned in the cellar.

Soon after Tuller had moved the troop to a different part of Limbo, the Streeters had become aware of the detachment of CeeDees entering Limbo and obviously heading for the spot where the three prisoners had been left. It was clear to everyone, at once, what had happened, and Stele angrily accused Tuller of treachery. A number of the other Streeters seemed just as troubled by the idea of their chief making a deal with the CeeDees. But Tuller pointed out that no *Streeters* had been betrayed and that the deal with the CeeDees would mean that the Streeters would be left in peace for a long time. That mollified most of the troop, despite how Stele, Rontal and Jeko felt.

But the following day a Streeter came to join the others from one of the sentry posts that were placed on the edges of Limbo. From her hiding place, the sentry had overheard two CeeDees talking, while they were checking on a sleazy bar. She had heard that a force of Crushers was being readied for an all-out assault on Limbo, to wipe out the Streeters forever.

That terrifying news brought Tuller's reign to a sudden and messy end.

"Somethin' just snapped," Rontal growled, "when they all knew that Tuller had sold you out for nothin'. Jeko an' me went for Tuller, an' Stele too. An' then it was like the whole troop joined in. They were all over him, fists an' blades an' everythin'."

"Next minute," Jeko said with fierce satisfaction, "ol' Tuller looked like he fell under a hovertank."

Stele then became chief of the Streeters and organized the troop for survival. He sent most of them out of Limbo, but took Rontal and Jeko and about fifty others to clean out the Streeters' store of arms—mostly stunner and ripper guns and some high explosives. On the way, they found that Cord and the girls had escaped from the cellar, but Stele had no time to worry about his friends' survival. By then the Crushers were moving into Limbo.

The main body of Streeters ran straight into that lethal attacking force and were either killed or captured. But Stele and his smaller party used all their knowledge of Limbo to elude the Crushers and finally went into hiding in another part of the city.

"We figured all we could do was make a last fight of it somewhere," Jeko said darkly.

But the Streeters had always kept in touch with some of the city's "straight" criminals, outside Limbo. From them Stele heard the news that four "rebels" from another planet had been captured—so Jeko and Rontal were convinced that their friends from Klydor were probably dead. Stele also learned that the Streeter prisoners, about a hundred of them, were to be taken to ColSec Central. And more questioning and bribery soon unearthed the route that they would follow.

"So we figured to break the others out, if we could," Stele said.

"It seemed as good a way as any to have that last fight," Rontal put in dryly.

Jeko laughed. "Never expected to find you folk. Never expected to get away so clean, either."

"We haven't got away," Lathan pointed out. "There's a whole ColSec fleet at the spaceport, which we have to get through somehow. And any minute now, someone is going to notice that we're not heading for ColSec Central any more."

But, astonishingly, no one did. Because of that reassuring report from the Crushers, it seemed that the authorities had more or less forgotten about the prisoners. The CeeDees were paying more attention to the search for Streeters, throughout the city. So the flyer hurtled on, unhindered, with the transporter thundering along the streets below.

But eventually, inevitably, a moment came when it seemed that their luck had run out.

A grumpy voice abruptly emerged from the flyer's communicator. "Flyer 141," it said. "Report. Where the hell are you?"

"That's us," Lathan muttered. He took a deep breath and reached for the communicator. "141 reporting. Escorting prisoners in transporter, as ordered." He was doing a fair imitation of the Crusher's cold voice, Cord realized. "We departed from original route, in case of further trouble. Estimate arrival at ColSec Central in about six minutes."

For a seemingly endless moment, they all held their breath. Then the grumpy voice replied.

"Acknowledged, 141. Don't take all day. Out."

The six of them sighed with relief, and Lathan grinned. "We'll be at the spaceport in half that time. Look ahead."

From their height, they found that they could see their goal—the vast spreading expanse of the city's main spaceport. And their nerves tautened again as they saw what awaited them.

The enormous breadth of concrete seemed packed with spacecraft, of every make and size, resting on every available landing pad. And the spaces among the ships were equally crowded, with uniformed people. Most of the uniforms were CeeDee blue, but many of them gleamed with silver and scarlet—the colours of ColSec's security forces.

A moment later, Lathan swung the flyer down towards the main gate. Glancing back, Cord saw the transporter barrelling along, less than a minute behind them. But then he looked ahead again, and a wash of icy sweat swept across his back.

From among the nearest ships, an oversized CeeDee floater, bristling with weapons, was curving swiftly towards the flyer as it settled to the ground.

14

Escape from Earth

Lathan looked at Cord. "You and I'll go out, since we're in uniform. But not with the sun-guns—they're Crusher weapons."

Rontal and Jeko happily took the weapons, and Samella accepted Jeko's gun—so that all four who would remain in the flyer would be armed.

"We'll try to talk our way in," Lathan went on. "But if they've been alerted..."

"Then we fight," Heleth said calmly.

"Win or lose," Jeko added. "Like all the best fights."

Tensely, Cord followed Lathan out of the flyer, to face the man emerging from the large floater. It was a ColSec officer, in bright silver and scarlet.

"I'm Commandant Mirvandel," he announced. "What's going on?"

"Trouble in the city, sir," Lathan said. "Streeters tried to free prisoners. A lot of them got away—and CeeDee Command reckons they might try something here."

"Here?" The commandant looked amazed. "They'd be insane. I have ten times the men I need to finish those scavengers."

"More men coming, too, sir," Lathan said. "A transporter is right behind us."

The commandant frowned. "More men? Hardly necessary. Still . . . You guide the transporter, in your flyer, over to the far perimeter of the 'port. Marshal the men there."

"Yessir!" Lathan said, as the commandant wheeled away. Cord could hear him barking confident orders, organizing the defence of the spaceport. Then he and Lathan were climbing back into the flyer, where the others were trying to stifle their wild laughter.

Lathan lifted the flyer, hovering above the gate as the transporter thundered into view. Cord leaned out of the flyer, beckoning to the startled Stele, indicating that the transporter should follow. Then Lathan swung the flyer away, the transporter keeping pace below.

"I don't believe it," Samella said slowly. "It seemed too easy."

"It's like I told you," Lathan said. "The CeeDees have ruled the city for so long that they can't *conceive* that they might be beaten. So they've grown sloppy and careless—and we should be grateful."

"We haven't beat them yet," Rontal growled.

"You said *six minutes* to that fell' on the communicator. Only about two of 'em left."

"It'll have to be enough," Lathan said quickly.

As the flyer soared on, Cord saw that few of the uniformed figures milling around the spaceport even glanced their way. Most of them were hurrying to take up their positions against the imagined Streeter attack. That struck the teenagers as hilarious—and then their laughter almost went out of control, as Lathan exclaimed with total astonishment at the sight that lay before them.

"Like they put it there just for us," he breathed.

It was a bulky spaceship with a rounded, humped profile—reminding Cord of the shuttle on which he and his friends had crashed on Klydor, but far larger. It rested on a pad near the perimeter fence, set apart from the other spacecraft, with no CeeDees within a hundred metres of it.

"ColSec personnel shuttle," Lathan said. "It'll hold us all, easily."

"Why is it over here?" Samella asked. "Maybe there's something wrong with it."

Lathan shook his head. "It's not part of the ColSec fleet, because it doesn't have faster-than-light drive. It was probably used to bring some of these men here."

The flyer landed next to the bulk of the giant shuttle, and the transporter swung up beside it. They all looked back, but still saw no sign of any attention aimed at them.

"If the shuttle doesn't have FTL drive," Samella

was objecting, "how can we use it? Any of these other ships could catch us long before we get to Klydor."

Lathan was thinking hard. "Then we won't go to Klydor," he said. "If we take off quickly, we'll have a head start—we'll be out in deep space before any ship can get men on board and lift off after us. By the time they do, we'll be out of scanner range. Then we'll head for the *asteroid*—and call for help."

Cord blinked, then remembered that while he and his friends had been landing on Earth, another rebel group had been setting up a temporary base within an asteroid, to assemble the recruits for the Klydor army.

"You mean get the rebel ships to come pick us up?" Rontal asked.

As Lathan nodded, Samella frowned doubtfully. "They could lock a computer on to the shuttle, like they did with your ship, and track us all the way to the asteroid."

Lathan shrugged. "Maybe. But maybe not, if we take them by surprise, and if our luck stays good. I know it's risky—but it's the only chance we have."

"Let's do it, then!" Heleth said sharply. "If ColSec follows us to the asteroid, we'll just have to hold them off till the rebels get to us!"

Jeko laughed, patting his sun-gun. "Sounds good. I was hopin' for a chance to use this."

"You might get one, 'bout now," Rontal cut in. "We got trouble."

They all whirled, staring out of the window.

The horde of uniformed men was no longer milling around. It was surging purposefully across the concrete, with the ColSec commandant's large floater in the lead—heading directly for the shuttle.

"Somebody woke up!" Lathan snapped, as they flung themselves out of the flyer.

Cord saw that the huge force of men would overwhelm them in less than a minute. But it was all the time they needed. Stele and the Streeters were already boiling out of the transporter, as Lathan sprang to open the shuttle's broad airlock. In seconds, a hundred and fifty Streeters had poured into the shuttle, swift and organized and without panic. At the same time, Rontal and Jeko directed a blaze of sun-gun fire at the advancing forces, scattering them in a confused search for cover.

Then they were all in the shuttle, and the huge ship trembled with the ignition of its engines. The enemy had time only to fire a few wild shots as the shuttle lifted, its thunder almost rivalled by the wild yell of exultation that echoed around its interior.

Within moments they had blasted out into the starry blackness of space. As the Streeters stared out of the viewports with silent awe, Cord and his friends clustered at the control panel, where Lathan was adjusting the communicator to call the rebel leaders on the planet Itharac. Soon he was outlining, to startled listeners on that world, what had been happening and what they were planning.

The voice from the communicator seemed to be

trying to control amazed laughter. "We'll send ships for you," it said. "But it'll take us two days to reach the asteroid. By then you and your friends will probably have finished off ColSec by yourselves."

The teenagers grinned at each other. "Have you destroyed the colonies and evacuated yet?" Lathan asked.

"Most of them," the voice said. "We started as soon as you went missing. We thought ColSec would learn all our plans—but there's been no sign of them out here."

"They haven't been hurrying," Lathan said. "They still don't know that the colonists have anywhere else to go, or any ships to go in."

The voice chuckled. "Everything is set on Klydor to surprise them. We picked up the Highlanders and Bunker kids from the asteroid, no trouble. Quite a little army—not many of them, but tough."

"We've got a hundred and fifty Streeters here," Lathan said, "to add to it. If you come and get us in time."

"We'll do our best," the voice said. "See you then."

Lathan flicked the communicator off. "Now we head for the asteroid—and wait."

"And hope," Samella said edgily.

The shuttle plunged forward through the emptiness, hour upon hour. And though it lacked the interplanetary FTL drive, its speed was impressive enough. Before too much longer, the Asteroid Belt appeared on the scanner screens—and the rear scanners showed no signs of pursuit.

Soon they were curving down towards the asteroid that was their goal—an immense chunk of bare and cratered rock. As the shuttle descended, Cord saw a pair of enormous doors that seemed to be set into the surface of the asteroid.

"Our entrance," Lathan said. "A giant airlock that opens automatically. Transport shuttles go inside the asteroid, to pick up loads of ore."

The mighty doors yawned open and the shuttle dropped gently through them, coming to rest in a huge, dimly lit area underground. As the great doors closed, atmosphere was restored to that section of the interior, hollowed out by decades of ColSec mining. The shuttle's airlock opened, and everyone poured out through it.

Cord paused, staring around, almost staggered by what he saw. He had expected something like a large cavern, but was unprepared for the sheer size of it. On every side lay a rugged, broken terrain of rock, glinting darkly from artificial lights spotted at widely spaced intervals. So much of the asteroid's interior had been carved away that Cord could not see the dome-like roof above, or the far walls of the open area. He felt that he might be standing on a rocky plain just about anywhere.

He shivered a little, not from cold but from the feeling of the place—the desolate bareness of the rock, with the expanses of inky darkness made even blacker by contrast with the scattered pools of stark white light. As they moved away, Cord soon glimpsed some of the mining robots—small, broad machines with metal extensor arms, looking as weird and alien as the rest of the place.

Before too long, they came to the buildings of the mining installation—a cluster of box-like structures made of plain plastic and metal. The area around the buildings was fairly well lit, but seemed silent and uninhabited.

"The others cleared up well," Lathan murmured. Cord too was surprised to see no sign that the other group of rebels had briefly taken over the asteroid.

Swiftly they checked the buildings and found them deserted—including the sleeping quarters for the asteroid's small staff of humans, who had also been taken to Klydor by the rebels, so they could not alert ColSec after the rebels had left. Other buildings housed workshops and repair shops and the giant motors—akin to a spaceship's engines—that powered the life support and all the other automatic systems. Finally, Lathan and Cord and his friends entered the central control building—a single open area like a warehouse, crammed with complex computer equipment that controlled all the robots and the other automated technology of the installation.

Samella's eyes brightened. "I could get to like this place," she said. "This stuff is really advanced."

"Enjoy yourself," Lathan said. "We'll be here for a while."

"We're all enjoying this," Stele said cheerfully. "It's a lot more fun than Limbo."

"You'll like Klydor better," Cord told him. "Even if ColSec attacks."

"*'Specially* if ColSec attacks," Jeko added.

Still chatting, the group moved away to look more closely at the high-tech equipment. But Cord, mystified as ever by technology, moved to one of the small windows, staring out at the bleak rock. He still felt almost dazed by the violent swiftness of their escape from Earth, and the unbelievable good fortune that had accompanied it. He could hardly believe that, earlier in the same day, he and his friends were on their despairing way to an interrogation, a trial and an execution. Now they were safe in space and only two days away from being taken home, to Klydor.

It would not be easy, he knew, to wait through those two days before the rebel ships reached them. He was filled with a terrible hunger for Klydor and the freedom it represented. And he was also filled with a fierce eagerness for the moment when he and his friends, and Stele's Streeters, would add their number to the Klydorean force that would confront—and possibly defeat—the might of ColSec.

Lost in such thoughts, Cord only slowly grew aware that something had changed in the atmosphere of the equipment-filled room around him. Everyone seemed to have gone very still, and all talk had ended. Turning, he saw them standing, white-faced, staring at one of the bright screens among the banks of complex technology.

Part of his mind told Cord that it looked like a

scanner screen, keeping watch on space beyond the asteroid. But the rest of his mind had been abruptly emptied of all thought.

The screen revealed a number of moving points of light. Moving in *formation*, creating the pointed shape of a triangle—or a spearhead—on the screen. There seemed to be about twenty-five points of light in the formation. And they were growing steadily larger as he watched.

He needed no one to tell him what they were. They had to be some of the ships from the ColSec fleet. Twenty-five ships full of armed men—storming through space on a direct course for the asteroid.

15

War on the Asteroid

"Looks like our luck ran out at last," Samella said quietly.

"Got here quick, didn't they?" Rontal said.

Lathan stared emptily at the screen. "They must have tracked us with a computer after all, as we lifted off. *Someone* wasn't sloppy or careless at that spaceport. And those ships will hold over six hundred men."

"So you get to have your last fight, just like you said," Heleth said to Stele. "Up here."

Stele shrugged. "Good a place as any."

"Sure," Jeko said, his eyes glittering. "And maybe some of us can hold out till the rebels get here."

I wouldn't count on it, Cord thought to himself grimly—not against six hundred men. But he kept silent. He was slightly surprised at the matter-of-fact reaction of his friends, but he was just as surprised at his own reaction. The first rush of icy dread, at the sight of the ColSec ships on the screen, had passed quickly. Perhaps he had become so used to danger and despair, he thought, that this newest and undoubtedly final disaster had little effect. And anyway, they might have expected their astonishing run of luck to come to an end sometime. But the risk, like all their risks, had had to be met. Once they had taken the shuttle, the asteroid was the only place they could have gone.

He grinned tightly as Samella gave him one of her wry, crooked smiles. As usual, he wished that she was somewhere else, safe. But at the same time he felt a kind of bitter gladness that the five of them would be together at the end.

Jeko nudged Rontal. "If we can do good here, maybe the fight on Klydor'll go easier."

"If there is one," Rontal said. "The rebels could still make ColSec back off, like they planned."

"Exactly," Lathan put in. "I still feel that ColSec isn't going to fight a major war in space, once they see that the rebels have spaceships and are ready for them." He smiled bleakly. "But that won't help us here."

Listening to them, Cord began to feel a strange exhilaration welling up within him, an eagerness for this last, hopeless battle. That was what it was about, he thought. If we can't fight and die *on*

Klydor, it's just as good to be able to fight and die *for* Klydor.

"I better get the Streeters organized, spread them out in all these rocks," Stele said, and laughed. "Won't seem much different from Limbo, for fighting."

He turned to the door, with Rontal and Jeko following, hefting their sun-guns. Cord gathered up his own sun-gun, as Heleth—carrying the fourth of the powerful weapons that they had taken from the Crushers—hurried after the Streeters. "Just save me a nice *dark* place," she was saying as she went out.

Lathan glanced once more at the screen, where the ColSec force was no longer a formation of points of light, but clearly defined spacecraft. "They'll land in a few minutes," he said.

"Couldn't we block those big doors somehow?" Cord suggested.

"It wouldn't work," Lathan said. "They'll land on the surface and come in wearing spacesuits. They could blast through the entrance in seconds." He began to turn away. "You two coming?"

Cord began to follow, but was halted by Samella's voice.

"I'll stay here for a while," she said. Her voice sounded strange, as if most of her thoughts were somewhere else.

Cord looked at her curiously. "What for?"

"I'm not really sure, yet," she said abstractedly.

"I have a sort of an idea... and I want to stay and think about it for a minute. You two go ahead."

Lathan moved out of the door, but Cord hesitated, frowning. "I'll stay with you," he decided.

Samella smiled. "Good," she said. "It'll be like when we met."

For a moment they looked at each other in silence, remembering their first meeting—in the small shuttle, during their initial flight to Klydor, when the two of them waited together for the crash-landing that they thought would probably kill them. Full circle, Cord thought—waiting for death again, together. But at least we had those months between then and now.

Then Samella smiled her crooked smile and turned away, and Cord moved to take up a position by a window, his sun-gun ready. Behind him, he was vaguely aware that Samella was bending over one of the banks of computer equipment, as absorbed and calm as if she were in some peaceful laboratory, rather than in the middle of what would soon be a short and bloody war. Then Cord fixed his attention on to the bleak bare rock outside his window. He felt his battle-eagerness returning and with it a strange alert coolness. He was faintly smiling as he gazed steadily in the direction of the huge entrance, from which the ColSec forces would soon appear.

Then his smile faded and his jaw clenched. The building had trembled slightly under his feet, as a heavy vibration throbbed through the rocky ground. And Cord did not need to know about advanced technology to understand the cause of that vibration.

The ColSec ships had landed on the asteroid.

It seemed a long time—a time of endless silent waiting and watching, which tested Cord's new coolness to the full—before he heard the first faint, distant clattering of metal and thud of booted feet. But there was no mistaking those noises. The ColSec force— hundreds of men, if Lathan's estimate had been right—were pouring into the asteroid's interior.

Cord jumped. The silence had been shattered by the faraway hiss of a laserifle and a hollow, muffled scream.

The battle had begun. Cord could imagine what was happening. The Streeters would have been scattered in good defensive positions among the rocks—and some of them had clearly set up an ambush, to fire on the enemy as they came through the entrance.

More firing followed at once—lasers, the electrical stunners, the evil ripper guns that fired minigrenades, all from the Streeters' substantial arsenal. But those sounds were overwhelmed by a sudden crashing thunder, and the distant darkness was slashed apart by lurid bursts of brilliance.

The ColSec forces were firing back at last, unleashing the ferocious power of hundreds of sunguns. The cavernous interior of the asteroid echoed with the almost continuous roar and the crashing collapse of shattered rock. The enemy firepower was terrifying—and their response to the Streeter attack left no doubt in Cord's mind how this battle would end.

Yet he did not shift, in his crouch by that window, nor did his expression change. Even the sight of that awesome enemy onslaught and the knowledge that his side was probably outnumbered six to one did not lessen his battle-readiness. There would be a lot of fighting to do before the inevitable end. And for all the ColSec numbers and weaponry, they were fighting Streeters—guerrilla warriors who knew all about lurking in shadowed ambushes, striking hard and then fading away before the counterattack.

In the distance the initial burst of firing died away. The silence that followed was broken by the unexpected boom of an amplified voice, resonating within the vast cavern.

"Attention!" the voice said. "This is ColSec Commandant Mirvandel!"

Cord recognized the voice of the confident officer who had let them into the spaceport. He grinned to himself as he heard the barely concealed fury in the man's voice.

"You have no chance of survival or escape," Mirvandel's amplified voice boomed. "I have a force of seven hundred armed men. If you wish to leave this asteroid alive, throw down your weapons and come out."

"So we can go back to Earth to be killed?" shouted a voice that sounded like Stele, from the darkness.

"Tell you what, commandant!" yelled another voice that was certainly Jeko's. "You throw *your* guns down and come out!"

The expanse of shadowy rock echoed with a wild burst of Streeter laughter. And it was followed at once by another torrent of firing from the defenders—mingling with howls from the ColSec forces, some of whom had clearly grown careless during the exchange of words.

But then again the asteroid reverberated with the deafening roar of hundreds of sun-guns, as the ColSec forces struck back.

Cord did not move. His half-smile had reappeared. He had enjoyed Stele's and Jeko's replies to Mirvandel's absurd order and had fully shared in the Streeter response. Was the ColSec officer really so arrogant that he could believe that any Streeters would surrender, to be tamely taken back to Earth and face execution? It was as if Mirvandel could not conceive of the existence of people who would rather die fighting.

I wonder what Mirvandel would do, in our position, Cord thought.

He was still peering out of the window, straining to penetrate the darkness ahead. He did not want to shoot at shadows, for fear they might be Streeters on the move. And it was clear to him that the Streeters were moving. By then the bursts of gunfire were growing more sporadic and scattered, as the ColSec forces spread out through the asteroid. And the sound of battle was drawing nearer. The enemy was steadily pushing forward, driving the Streeters back step by grudging step, no doubt reducing their numbers even further as they did so.

It would be only a matter of minutes before that steamroller advance would reach Cord's position.

16

Ultimatum

Briefly Cord glanced back, to see that Samella was probing deeply into the bowels of a computer console, seeming as untroubled as before by the battle raging nearby. Cord could not imagine what she was doing—but she was safe where she was, for the moment. And she would stay safe, Cord told himself fiercely, for as long as he was on his feet and breathing.

He turned back to the window, bracing himself, finger poised over the sun-gun's firing stud. And then a frightening thought struck him. What if an advance group of CeeDees had already got that far, and was approaching the building from another direction?

He flung himself across the room and opened the door to the building, a narrow crack. His heart almost stopped as he saw that his fear, perhaps a warning from some warrior instinct, had been proved right. Three dark-blue figures were creeping through the rocks, not far away from the building. They looked peculiar—and Cord realized that they were not in CeeDee uniform as on Earth but in differently shaped, light combat spacesuits.

A cold and flinty anger swelled within him, wholly unlike his usual fighting fury. He seemed hardly to take aim before his sun-gun's blast struck out and cut two of the CeeDees down where they stood. The third had time to turn and try to flee but toppled with a screech as the flame of Cord's gun slashed across his legs.

Before that CeeDee hit the ground, Cord was diving back across the room, to peer again out of the window. He saw a glint of metal, many metres away, recognized it as a dark-blue helmet, and fired in the same instant. Splinters of rock fountained up where the helmet had been. For several moments Cord watched that spot, tensely, but the helmet did not reappear. At last he turned, hurtling back again to his position by the door.

Among the rocks beyond the central building, the battle was still raging—the mighty thunder of sun-guns drowning all the sounds of the Streeter resistance. If, Cord thought, there were any Streeters still alive and resisting. It occurred to him that he and Samella, in their building, might sometime soon be among the last living members of their small, outnumbered force.

Pushing that thought away, he sprang back to

the window. Again there was no immediate sign of an enemy. But Cord was beginning to have doubts about his strategy. He could not go on trying, alone, to defend two or more entrances. He could easily end up holding off one attack from the window while another CeeDee group made an assault on the door.

He glanced again at Samella, now half-hidden in the depths of another large console. He was reluctant to leave her, but he knew that was because of an emotional wish to be with her when he was finally killed. And reason told him that it made more sense to go out of the building—where he could use his outdoor skills to slip unseen among the rocks, all around the building, and pick off any CeeDees who got too close.

As the thought formed, he put it into action, leaping for the door. A quick glance outside showed that the rocks beyond seemed empty of enemies. Without hesitation he flung himself out of the building, in a headlong sprint towards the nearest cover.

But he was only halfway across the distance when he saw the glitter of a silver and scarlet spacesuit, to his right—and knew that he had no chance.

Though he was fully exposed, he tried to stop his hurtling rush in time to bring his sun-gun to bear. But the ColSec man had already taken aim. At the last instant Cord dived desperately forward, full-length, feeling the searing heat as the fiery blast scorched over his head. He tried to roll aside, knowing that there was no way he could escape the enemy's second shot.

The sun-gun thundered. But to Cord's utter astonishment, as he lay there in the gritty dirt, he remained totally unscathed. Jerking his head up, he saw the ColSec man falling, the front of the bright spacesuit shattered and ablaze.

Then Cord heard a cheerful yell and dazedly saw Jeko rise from a heap of rocks ten metres away, with Rontal and Stele beside him.

"Good move, Cord!" Jeko called mockingly. "You run around in the open and draw 'em so we can pick 'em off!"

"Once was enough!" Cord shouted and dashed in among the rocks to join them.

"Glad you could make it," Rontal said with a grin. "Samella all right?"

Cord grimaced. "She's doing something with the computers—don't ask me what. I thought I'd do better out here, moving around the building."

"Makes sense," Rontal drawled. "Whatever that girl's doin', I reckon it's important. Se we better make sure she goes on doin' it awhile."

"Where's Heleth?" Cord asked.

"Went lookin' for a real dark place," Jeko said. "Lathan went with her, 'cause you know she can't see for a coupla minutes after firin' a sun-gun." His mouth twisted. "We could sure do with a few more Bunker folk in here."

"We could do with . . ." Stele began.

But then all talk ended.

The rocks ahead of them suddenly seemed to be swarming with blue spacesuits. A contingent of CeeDees was making a concerted rush against the computer building—and as far as Cord could tell, only he and the three Streeters stood in their way.

Cord was the first to fire, as the others fanned out to meet the CeeDee charge. There seemed to be an incredible number of blue spacesuits, their guns pouring out a fury of flame. Cord's gun grew warm in his hands as he fired again and again, dodging behind rocks, leaping up to continue the firing. He grew deafened by the blasts from his own gun and from those of his friends around him. He hardly noticed the chunks of shattered rock flying around him from enemy blasts, hardly noticed the piercing pain as a flaming bolt grazed his shoulder like a knife-slash. He fired and fired, not stopping even when Stele spun and fell limply, when Jeko's shirt seemed to burst into flame as another bolt struck him, when Rontal toppled as flame scythed across his legs. The roaring of the sun-guns seemed to blend into a roaring in Cord's ears, and from somewhere he imagined he could hear the bloodthirsty howl of Highland pipes, summoning all of his wild, stubborn courage. Still he fired, endlessly, ferociously, half-blindly . . .

Until with startling suddenness he saw that there were no more blue spacesuits in sight to fire at.

He slumped, feeling drained of energy. The next attack, he thought wearily—that will finish us, no question. He could still hear the battle raging elsewhere among the rocks, but the firing sounded even more sporadic now. Either the Streeters were staying in cover, making themselves hard to find, or there were only a few of them left to be found.

But some of his energy and battle-hunger was restored when he saw his friends stirring. Jeko had just been grazed and had suffered only minor burns from his flaming shirt. Rontal sat up and began calmly binding the dripping wound in one leg. And even Stele raised himself slowly to a sitting position, clutching a shattered shoulder with a faintly puzzled expression.

Cord glanced at his own wound indifferently, seeing that the bleeding had almost stopped. Then he straightened, taking a deep breath.

"I'm going to circle the building," he told the others. "They could be sneaking up on the other side."

"Come back if you can," Jeko replied with a ghost of his grin. "The next attack's gonna be the big one. You wouldn't wanta miss it."

Cord nodded, trying to think of something suitable to say. Before he could speak, he was almost deafened by a new outburst of sound.

It was not a renewed attack upon them. It was a human voice, amplified just as the ColSec commandant's had been. But it was coming from the building that they were defending.

Samella's voice.

"Commander Mirvandel! All of you! Hold your fire and listen to me!"

"How's she doin' that?" Jeko asked excitedly.

"*What's* she doin' is the question," Rontal said, as the firing in the asteroid died away to leave a startled silence.

"Listen carefully," Samella went on, her steady voice rolling out through the darkness. "I'm speaking from the central control building of this installation. It's the nerve centre of all the technology here—including the power source."

Cord saw a doubt-filled realization dawning on Rontal's face. "She *couldn't . . .*" he murmured.

"I have reprogrammed the computers controlling the power source," Samella's voice continued into the now breathless silence. "The new programme has overriden all safety precautions and has brought the power source almost to critical overload. I need to press only *one key*—and the power source will explode." She paused. "A nucleonic fusion explosion, Mirvandel, which will turn this asteroid into radioactive dust."

The next pause was also relatively short, but Cord felt himself ageing rapidly through it. Then the ColSec commandant replied, using his own amplified speaker.

"You're bluffing," Mirvandel bellowed. "You couldn't possibly do what you say!" An audible sneer entered his voice. "And I don't believe you would wipe out all your *friends*!"

Samella's calm tone did not alter. "My name is Samella Connel," she replied. "ColSec will have a record of my computer training—you can check it easily. As for my friends, since they're about to be wiped out anyway, I think they'd be happy to take you with them." Her voice rose slightly. "Right, Streeters?"

The reply seemed as thunderous as a hundred sun-guns. *"Right!"* the surviving Streeters yelled, with Cord and the three next to him shouting as loud as any. That roar was followed by separate, scattered yells. "You tell 'em, chuck!" "Do it, girl!" "Blow 'em away!"

"There's your answer, Mirvandel," Samella's voice said flatly. "Your men can't reach me before I press this key. If I do, you and your men die—and ColSec loses twenty-five spacecraft and a very expensive mining installation. Think about it, commandant."

Silence fell again, even deeper than before. In the midst of it, while Cord almost had to keep reminding himself to breathe, he heard a faint rustle nearby. He whirled, his gun coming up—but relaxed as a familiar giggle came from the darkness.

"Just me," Heleth said, stepping out from the rocks with Lathan close behind. "Thought we'd better come back, now that Samella's doing so good by herself."

"It's incredible," Lathan said. "I'd never have guessed that those computers could be overriden."

"She *could* be bluffing," Heleth said softly.

That thought had occurred to Cord as well and had not eased his tension. "If she is," he said, "and Mirvandel calls the bluff, we'll be no worse off."

"Meanin' we go back to fightin' till they get us," Jeko said with something like relish.

But at last Mirvandel had come to the point where he could reply. And he sounded agonized by the decision being forced upon him.

"I don't believe any of it!" he yelled. "You can't do what you said! You *can't!*"

His voice broke on the last word, and Cord and his friends grinned at each other.

"I can and I have," Samella said coolly. "Why don't you go to your ship and contact ColSec Central, Mirvandel? You can check on me, and you can present *them* with the choice. Either you order your men to surrender—which means that you and they and all of ColSec's valuable ships and equipment remain intact. Or"—her voice darkened—"you order your men to commit suicide."

"Brilliant!" Lathan said. "That could push the CeeDees close to mutiny!"

Mirvandel made no reply. But they all heard something like a muffled curse from the ColSec officer's speaker, before it was shut off. And another wait, the longest by far, began.

Perhaps the CeeDee forces did grow close to mutiny, in the face of the threat of annihilation. Perhaps Mirvandel did contact his ColSec superiors, to find out just how skilled Samella was with microtronics. Perhaps ColSec Central, and not Mirvandel, made the decision finally about the fate of seven hundred men and a great deal of very valuable technology.

However it happened, eventually the decision was made. And the first indication of it, for the surviving defenders, was a widespread metallic clatter—which sounded oddly like a great number of sun-guns being thrown, unceremoniously, on to bare rock.

Then, with open-mouthed amazement and a soaring delight, Cord and the others watched as the enemy emerged. Group by group, they trudged into open areas, arms raised, hands empty, faces filled with anger and hatred and quite a bit of fear. They crowded together finally in one large mass, with Mirvandel pale and bowed in their midst. And the surviving Streeters surrounded them, weapons levelled—though the ColSec force seemed more disturbed by their mocking laughter than their guns.

Lathan hurried away to help organize the prisoners. But Cord and his friends had thoughts for only one thing. With Jeko and Heleth helping the more seriously injured Rontal and Stele, they raced into the computer building.

Samella was sitting at a computer console, her grey eyes exultant. Cord scooped her up into a mighty bear-hug, while she gasped with breathless laughter. Then he set her down and stared seriously into her eyes.

"You *weren't* bluffing, were you?" he asked.

She shook her head, smiling. "I wouldn't have had the nerve. It's just like I said—all set to blow up the asteroid."

"How'd you do the voice?" Rontal asked.

"Some of the computers have voices, like GUIDE,"

Samella said. "I borrowed their speakers and amplifiers and linked them together."

"And it woulda needed just one key to blow us away," Jeko said wonderingly. "Which one? This?"

His finger stabbed down at the keyboard. But as the others yelled, he twitched his finger aside at the last second, laughing deliriously.

His laughter stopped as Rontal's hand clamped painfully around his throat. "Y'know," Rontal growled, "there's times I reckon Heleth's right. You *are* a yeck-head."

That set them all off, and they were weak with laughter when Lathan walked in.

"Nothing funnier than victory?" he asked dryly.

"Nothing sweeter, anyway," Cord said.

"Don't start celebrating too soon," Lathan replied. "We've won an important battle—but there still could be a war."

Cord's jaw tightened. "We were ready to fight ColSec before. We're still ready."

"And," Samella added, "we have twenty-five more ships and a few hundred more sun-guns to fight with."

"True," Lathan said soberly. "So perhaps now there's more of a chance that ColSec might realize—eventually—how crippling a war on Klydor could be, for them. It just depends on what price they're willing to pay, to try to crush us."

Stele, standing slightly apart, was looking thoughtful. "Wouldn't it make sense," he asked, "to *show* them what they would face, if they attack us? If they knew about the rebel ships and the army on Klydor *before* they send out the rest of their fleet..."

"They might not send it at all," Heleth said excitedly.

Lathan blinked, then smiled. "That's a thought," he said. "Maybe we should give ColSec our ultimatum as soon as the rebel ships come to pick us up. And we could take some of our ColSec prisoners to Klydor—maybe Mirvandel—and show them all the rebel preparations, then send them back to Earth to report."

"That should make ColSec stop and think," Samella said.

Jeko's irrepressible laughter burst out. "We don't need ol' Mirvandel for that," he chortled. "There's a coupla missin' ColSec *inspectors* who'd be glad to do that job!"

17

Pathfinders

The breeze had a crisp bite to it, as the Klydorean autumn deepened towards winter. But the orange sun sill offered its warmth at midday, and Cord and his four friends were sprawled comfortably out of the wind, on the turf-clad banks of the pool near which they had captured the two ColSec inspectors.

In fact Cord and his *five* friends were lounging there, for next to Samella rested the small metal case of GUIDE, the computer, who seemed none the worse for his time of isolation on Klydor.

But isolation, on that world, was now a thing of the past, unless it was sought purposefully. In the distance the friends could hear the shouts and clatter of other teenagers, hard at work erecting a number of compact little houses against the coming winter. The structures were built mostly with local materials, including stone quarried by the Bunker Vampires from the cave-riddled badlands where they made their home, and lumber from nearby forested hills where the Highlanders had made themselves comfortable.

Cord glanced over at the busy scene of construction. "We ought to get back to work."

"Work," Jeko grumbled, scratching the light bandages on his burned torso. "Nobody has any fun here any more."

"Come visit the caves with me," Heleth said teasingly. "Lots of fun there."

Rontal stretched, easing his heavily bandaged leg. "Trouble with Jeko, he's an *action* junkie. Gotta look for trouble. Can't get used to all this peace."

That was the word, Cord thought happily. Peace—and freedom—had come to Klydor, and to all the colony worlds. A peace won through the prolonged and tense negotiations that had gone on with ColSec.

But there had been a time, earlier, when peace had seemed an extremely unlikely prospect...

The rebel ships had arrived at the asteroid in good time, and their pilots had been stunned by what they found there. At once all the Streeters had been whisked back to Klydor, along with the twenty-five ships—each flown by a ColSec pilot under heavy Streeter guard. The rest of the ColSec force, including the unhappy Mirvandel, was left on the asteroid to be collected in due course, since the rebels had no wish to be burdened with hundreds of prisoners.

Lathan and the five teenagers had taken a different route to Klydor—via Itharac, where they retrieved the two inspectors, Muril and Reema, and their CeeDee companions from the bleak area where they had been marooned. Then, on Klydor, Lathan took the inspectors on a grim guided tour of the rebels' preparations, and the now enlarged rebel spacefleet, before despatching them to Earth in their own ship.

After that, the rebels waited for ColSec's response. ColSec did not keep them waiting long.

Two days later, one of the orbiting sentry ships spotted, on the screens of its long-range scanners, the approach of a sizeable number of spacecraft. The ColSec fleet was hurtling vengefully towards Klydor.

On the planet, all activity seemed to come to a standstill, as if time itself had been suspended for a moment by that dire news. Lathan seemed especially stricken by this final end to hope—the hope that ColSec might see sense, might draw back from the costliness and pointlessness of a war in space. Now it seemed that ColSec and the Organization were willing to pay any price, no matter how crippling, to crush the rebellion.

Yet, as Cord had said before, the rebels had always been prepared to fight, and they were still prepared. They rallied their courage and determination, and their spaceships stormed into the sky to intercept the ColSec fleet. Lathan was flying the lead ship, and the five teenagers were with him, having refused to be left behind.

It was another time of nerve-twisting tension, as the two forces flashed towards each other. The ColSec fleet numbered more than sixty ships, while the rebels could muster only about thirty-five. Yet tension seemed to be affecting ColSec as well. Their ships began to lose speed, as if hesitating in the face of the armed rebel vessels confronting them.

"Looks like their confidence has been shaken a little," Lathan said with some satisfaction. "Let's see if they have anything to say."

He touched the communicator, opening up a wide-frequency link between the ColSec fleet and the rebel ships. Calmly he informed the ColSec force that they were trespassing on the territorial space of the free planet Klydor, and were required to leave at once.

The voice that replied identified itself as a High Marshal of the Civil Defenders. It was a sharp and snarling voice, shaking with barely controlled fury.

"You are in no position to make demands!" the marshal shouted. "You are *criminals*! You and all the scum on that planet will surrender, *now*, or we will wipe you out!"

"Marshal, you're a fool," Lathan replied icily. "We know that your ships outnumber ours two to one and that each of your ships is packed with armed men. But we *do not care*. We're going to fight you.

And even if you win, here in space, you'll lose many ships—because we'll fight to the death. So you'll have a smaller force to take down to the planet. Think about it, marshal. You'll have fewer men to land on a wild planet that you've never seen—where there could be a Streeter with a sun-gun behind every bush by day, and a Bunker Vampire in every shadow by night. Do you really think you can win that fight, marshal? Or would you rather calm down and talk, and work out a solution where neither we nor ColSec has to lose anything?"

The marshal's fury boiled over. *"Talk?"* His voice was rising to a near-hysterical scream. "There'll be no *talk!* When we're done, there'll be nothing left of you and your planet but *ashes!*"

"Perhaps," Lathan said flatly. "But by then there won't be much left of your force, either, to enjoy the victory. Doesn't anyone in ColSec understand what that victory will cost? You've already lost the colonies that we've destroyed, not to mention the expense of sending out your fleet. Can ColSec afford any more losses?"

There was a pause, during which Cord and the others could hear a strange spluttering noise, as if the marshal's rage had taken him beyond speech. Then another voice intervened, on the communicator. A hard, cold voice, which made Cord think of a north wind blowing over the ice-clad granite peaks of mountains.

"This is Galtry," the voice said. "I would be interested to know how you think this . . . situation

. . . can be resolved with neither side losing anything, as you put it. You rightly point out that we have already lost the colonies. If we punish you for that, as we surely can, you will lose everything."

Lathan turned startled eyes to the teenagers. "Galtry is the Director of ColSec," he muttered. "The top man—and one of the most powerful people in the Organization. If he's here . . ."

"They must be willing to talk," Samella finished.

Lathan nodded. "Or at least to consider the possibility." He took a deep breath and turned back to the communicator.

"I can answer you quite simply, director," he said. "If you try to 'punish' us, we will *not* lose everything—because we have nothing to lose. So we'll fight to the bitter end, if we have to. And by then ColSec will have lost far more than it already has." He hurried on before the director could reply. "There's a business phrase you should remember, director. About 'cutting your losses'. Yes, we destroyed the colonies. But who could *rebuild* them more quickly and cheaply—the people who created them in the first place, or groups of newcomers with no experience, who would have to be shipped out, expensively, to alien planets they've never seen?"

The communicator hummed softly during the silence that followed. Then the chill voice of Director Galtry replied.

"What would be your demands," he said, "in return, if we agree that you should begin that rebuilding?"

In the background, somewhere on the ColSec ship, Cord heard what sounded like a muffled shriek of rage and a scuffle, both rapidly silenced. But he paid little attention, for Lathan had turned to them with pure delight flaring in his eyes.

"They're *going to talk,*" he breathed.

"Sounded like the marshal's kinda disappointed," Rontal drawled.

"I know how he feels," Jeko said sourly. "I was lookin' forward to another fight."

But, instead, to the joyous relief of Cord and his friends and every person among the rebels, the negotiations began.

It soon became clear, though no one in ColSec ever admitted it, that a fierce argument had been raging within the top levels of the Organization. One group had insisted that the rebellion must be put down, at any cost, to protect the Organization's power. That group, including the CeeDee High Marshal, stubbornly believed that the rebellion would collapse in panic at a powerful show of force. And so the spacefleet had been sent to Klydor.

But the other group, which included Director Galtry, had been more concerned to protect the Organization's wealth. Coldly and logically, they were unwilling to add more losses to those which ColSec had already suffered. And so Galtry had gone with the fleet, prepared to begin talks with the rebels if the show of force did not panic them into giving up.

In short, ColSec had added up the realities. And at the end greed won over pride and forced it to accept those realities. The ship-to-ship negotiations, in space, lasted for some days, and were often bitter and resentful and angry. But slowly, inevitably, an agreement was hammered out.

The rebels agreed to rebuild the colonies, and to restart the flow of wealth from those worlds to Earth. And ColSec agreed to pay much fairer prices for the colonies' produce and to grant the colony worlds their freedom, with a guarantee that they would be left in peace to make their lives as they wished.

And part of the reason Cord and his friends were relaxing by the pool on Klydor at this moment, instead of helping with the construction of houses, was that they were still recovering from the extensive celebrations that had followed the completion of that agreement.

"I keep wishin' I coulda seen that ol' marshal's face," Jeko was saying, with a merciless smile. "All that screamin' and yellin'. Almost felt sorry for him."

Rontal chuckled. "Real softhearted, you."

"Lathan says the marshal had a breakdown," Heleth put in. "Like lots of other folk in the Organization."

"They never thought they'd ever be challenged," Cord said quietly, "let alone beaten. They can't face the fact that we won."

"And there have been lots of arrests," Samella added. "The Organization went looking for scapegoats, someone to blame. So they've been putting officers and officials in prison. Like poor Mirvandel."

"Prisons'll be gettin' full," Rontal said. "I heard there's rumours goin' round Earth 'bout the rebellion, though the Organization's tryin' to keep it quiet. There'll be trouble stirrin' if folks get the idea into their heads that the Organization can be beat."

Samella nodded. "That may have helped make ColSec decide not to fight us. The Organization will need its armed forces on Earth, to keep order."

"There's a thing," Heleth said gleefully. "We could have started something that'll shake Earth free, someday."

They were silent for a moment, savouring those possibilities for the future.

"Whatever happens," Cord said at last, "one of the best things is that there'll be no more exiles. That any kids taken by the CeeDees on Earth will get sent *here*, not thrown away on wild planets."

"No more *scards*," Rontal growled fervently.

Jeko snorted. "This place is crowded enough already."

"It's a big world," Cord said with a laugh. "Right, GUIDE?"

"Thank you for activating me," the little computer said in its soft voice. "The planet Klydor can support a population in excess of 1.8 billion. The present population, including temporary visitors from other colony worlds, is 947. Approximately 86.72 per cent of Klydor's surface has not yet been explored..."

"All right," Jeko cut in. "Samella, you been fillin' him up with stuff again?"

Samella smiled. "He likes to have his data banks topped up. And he's right. There's a lot of Klydor that no one's ever seen."

"They will," Jeko muttered. "I heard Lathan and Stele talkin' about gettin' some floaters and doin' a survey. In a while, this whole place is gonna be settled. And that means *dull*."

Cord grinned. "Rontal's right—you are hooked on action."

"Sure," Jeko agreed. "It's how I lived most of my life. You *get* hooked. I really liked it when we were by ourselves here, never knowin' what might happen next, what might try to kill us. And I'll bet"—he glanced around at them intensely—"no matter what you all think about this peace and quiet now, you'll start feelin' the same way soon enough. I bet *you* been hooked, too, by all the danger and excitement and stuff we've had."

Another silence fell. Heleth and Rontal were nodding slowly. Samella was looking uneasy, as if finding that she could not argue with Jeko's statement even if she wanted to. And Cord was discovering within himself a realization that what Jeko had said was probably true. The peaceful process of settling Klydor was a fine thing—but Cord, the wild Highlander, had felt most at home on Klydor when it was a wild planet. How long would it be, after the planet was settled, before he began to feel restless and stifled?

"He may be right," Cord said at last.

"First time ever," Heleth growled.

"You're all looking serious," said a voice behind them. They turned to see Bren Lathan, accompanied by Stele whose damaged shoulder was still firmly encased in bandages.

"Been thinkin' 'bout the future," Rontal drawled.

"Jeko's been warning us," Samella added, "that we're going to find Klydor dull and boring after a while."

"That's very likely," Lathan said. "All the newcomers are going to be swept along by the excitement of a new world and making new lives. But you old Klydoreans..." He grinned. "Maybe you should join me and the other space explorers. Remember, we worked out a deal with ColSec, to keep on looking for new worlds that can support humans."

"That means bein' stuck inside spaceships all the time," Jeko said. "Not me." And the others shook their heads firmly.

"Lathan's joking," Stele told them. "He's come to talk to you about something different."

"Only a little different," Lathan said. "Because if the other explorers and I find new worlds, we've agreed that ColSec should establish colonies on them."

"But doing it *our* way," Stele put in, "with *volunteers*. We'll be bringing out hundreds of kids, from all the troops on Earth."

Lathan nodded. "And now ColSec has asked us—politely—if we'd take a close look at a new planet that was discovered shortly before the rebellion."

Cord and his friends sat up, eager and curious, as they began to guess what Lathan was getting at.

"We need to get a team together," Lathan went on, "to explore that planet on the ground. It's a fairly wild place—so while the team would be well equipped, they'd still need to be tough and experienced . . . and lucky."

Jeko whooped. "That's it! Just what we need—another bunch of monsters and stuff!"

Cord glanced around and saw that all of them were looking as excited as he was feeling. "I think you've got your team, Bren," he said.

Lathan grinned. "And you sure you wouldn't rather help Stele and the Streeters build their houses? Or help the Vampires clean up their caves?"

Rontal shook his head seriously. "We're off the streets now, outa Limbo. For Jeko an' me, this's our troop, right here."

"For me, too," Heleth said firmly.

Samella's eyes were shining. "It's just right! We'll stay together and be the pioneers, the pathfinders, like we were here on Klydor. And we can go on to other planets when we're finished on . . ." She paused. "Bren, has this new world got a name?"

"No," Lathan said. "You *pathfinders* can give it a name."

Cord's face lit up. "I know what to call it," he said. "Just so no one ever forgets that the colonies didn't win their freedom only through all the talking with ColSec—but won it as well in that one battle of the rebellion, on the asteroid. Let's call the planet . . . *Samella!*"

The others roared with delighted agreement, while Samella tried to protest. Then, boisterous with laughter and excitement, they all hurried across the sunlit turf of Klydor to get ready for whatever another wild alien world, and their brand-new futures, would offer them.

ABOUT THE AUTHOR

DOUGLAS HILL was raised in the backwoods of Canada in Prince Albert, Saskatchawan. "Its main claim to fame," he says, "is that it's the second coldest town in North America." The landscape of his childhood was one of vast plains and forests, snow-covered in winter but full of blazing sunshine in summer. "The backwoods of Canada were a great place to grow up in but a lousy place to be an adolescent," Douglas Hill says. "I was a dreamer. I devoured science fiction. Flash Gordon and Buck Rogers were major comic strips in the newspapers in those days, and I read every one." He left home at age seventeen to attend university, first in Saskatoon and then moving east to school in Toronto. At age twenty-three, he moved east again—to England. In 1963, Douglas Hill began reviewing science fiction for the London weekly, *Tribune*. He was for some years Literary and Arts editor of *Tribune*, but now spends his time writing and advising publishers. His books include The Last Legionary series, four books about Keill Randor, and *Young Legionary*, Keill's early adventures, as well as The Huntsman trilogy.

An Explosive Science Fiction Adventure

The ColSec Trilogy
by Douglas Hill

☐ *EXILES OF COLSEC* (25785-4 • $2.75)—They were outcasts from Earth, young rebels exiled against their will to a harsh and deadly planet filled with vicious aliens and monstrous creatures. To survive, they had to learn to trust one another, to join together. But their deadliest peril came from the world they'd left behind.

☐ *THE CAVES OF KLYDOR* (25929-6 • $2.75)—The rebels have found the key to survival. But in the danger-filled depths of the caves of Klydor, they found a mysterious stranger who would alter their destinies forever.

☐ *COLSEC REBELLION* (On sale November 15, 1986 • 26145-2 • $2.75)—The rebels have made Klydor their own. Now they have returned to the savage streets that spawned them to rally Earth's young to rebellion.

Buy all of the books in the *ColSec Trilogy*, on sale wherever Bantam Spectra Books are sold, or use the handy coupon below for ordering: